# TAVISTOCK GALLERIA

## SHORT HORROR STORIES FROM AMERICA'S RETAIL WASTELAND

HORROR STORIES

This is a work of fiction. Names, characters, businesses, places, events and incidents are either the products of the author's imagination or used in a fictitious manner. Any resemblance to actual persons, living or dead, or actual events is purely coincidental.

Tavistock Galleria
First Edition January 2019

PUBLISHING

Read More Horror
TobiasWade.Com

Copyright © 2019

All rights reserved. This book or any portion thereof may not be reproduced or used in any manner whatsoever without the express written permission of the publisher except for the use of brief quotations in a book review.

CONTENTS

1. Times Were Different Then — 1
2. Prom Dresses — 17
3. Tavistock After Dark — 33
4. Mall Walkers — 40
5. The Fountain — 49
6. Life in Retail — 58
7. Closing Day — 81
8. Fast Forward — 112
9. Retail Therapy — 122
10. Bitchcraft — 141
11. I Smelled Every One — 161
12. The Carousel of Tavistock Galleria — 167
13. Destination — 193
14. The End of Tavistock — 203
    Read More Horror — 223

Special thanks for

Desdymona Howard and her wonderful illustrations. You can find more of her work:

https://desdymona.wordpress.com/

And William Stuart for editing these stories.

https://www.amazon.com/William-Stuart/e/B07HHK2X5F

This book wouldn't be here without you.

TAVISTOCK GALLERIA

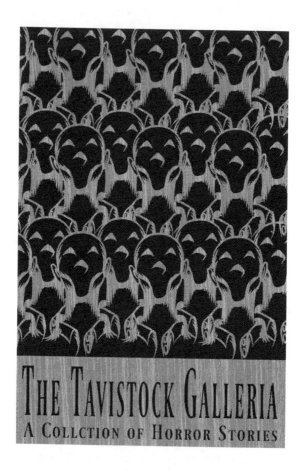

# TIMES WERE DIFFERENT THEN

By C.M. Scandreth

JOHNNY RAISIN WAS POOR AS SHIT, AND EVERYBODY KNEW IT. He lived with his mom in a trailer on the scrapyard—rent free, because their three mangy dogs kept the rats and kids away. They were hoarders of the worst sort, keeping everything that other people threw away. Stacked against the side of the trailer was a teetering wall of broken, one-wheeled bicycles and tricycles Johnny had collected over the years, streaked with rust and dog piss, like some half-completed Salvador Dali project.

There was so much junk inside the trailer itself it was hard to move without knocking something over. Johnny's mom was fifty if she was a day, and she complained bitterly about the cold, staying wrapped in a massive woolen blanket that hooked and snagged on every metal object in their home. It smelled in there too, like old dog food and bug spray; but Johnny had a PlayStation 3 that mostly worked even though the case was held together with tape. I didn't, so I spent more time in that stinking, cluttered trailer than I might have otherwise.

I wasn't using Johnny, I told myself. We'd been friends since kindergarten, and when the other kids picked on him, I always stood up for him. He was practically family—my parents let him come over and shower once a week and my mom would wash his threadbare clothes while dad cooked him waffles with maple and bacon. Johnny was the brother I'd never had, and I knew that if anything happened to his mom, we'd have adopted him in an instant. The only reason why he didn't live with us permanently was that we didn't want to hurt his mom's feelings.

"She does the best she can," my mom said, her forehead crinkled with empathy, "losing her man hurt her deeper than any of us can imagine."

So, Johnny Raisin stayed living in the junkyard—and honestly, he liked it that way, because he had more freedom than any other kid his age.

Johnny was always trying to make money at school by selling stuff to other kids. Not just his scrapyard treasures; he was an expert scavenger. He raided the lost property boxes at community halls and libraries, and walked around the streets with his head down, scanning for coins and dropped possessions. Most of what he found was garbage, but very occasionally he'd have a big win and sell something for twenty bucks. The rare times that happened, I'd know, because he'd promptly blow it all on candy and soda, making himself sick on all the luxuries he didn't often get.

So, when Johnny started showing up at school regularly with his backpack full of Milk Duds, Twinkies, Skittles and cans of Dr Pepper, all for sale, I didn't know what to make of it. The other kids eagerly bought the contraband, since

Johnny was asking a tenth of the retail price. They commented on the huge, old-school steel cans the soda came in, antiques from the 80s that Johnny had unearthed somewhere on his nocturnal roamings. I was wary of the long-expired products at first, but the food and drink tasted as good as if they'd been packaged last week, so I happily filled Johnny's pockets with coins too.

The mystery deepened when Johnny started turning up in new clothes. Well, technically they weren't new at all—they were relics from several decades ago, just like the soda cans. But the colours were crisp and bright, and the fabric still had packaging creases and smelled of plastic wrappers. When I raised my eyebrows at his 'Return of the Jedi' t-shirt, Johnny just grinned at me and jingled the coin-filled pockets of his red 'Beat It' era jacket. He looked like he'd stepped out of some old music video.

"Gonna go buy Fallout: New Vegas after school," he said, jerking a thumb in the direction of the mall, "wanna come?"

"You know I do," I told him, shouldering my backpack.

As we walked, Johnny whistled weirdly tuneless elevator music and checked his watch—also in theme, some decades-old Swatch model. I knew that he was playing it up on purpose; he knew I was desperate to find out where he'd been getting all this stuff, but I was damned if I was going to crack first and say anything.

"So. I've been exploring Tavistock Galleria, down by the lake," he said finally, breaking a full ten minutes of silence.

"Jesus, Johnny! That's where you've been getting all this stuff from?"

"Yup."

"But that place has been abandoned forever. There's nothing left in there."

Johnny just kept on grinning, giving me sidelong glances from beneath the brim of his vintage Laker's baseball cap, while I processed this information.

The Galleria had been the place to be, once upon a time. Back in the 70s, it had been the hub of the town—according to my mom. Kids would play ball in the park by the lake while parents shopped at their leisure, transported between the two mezzanine floors by fancy new escalators of shiny chrome and steel. A massive underground parking lot meant finding a spot for your car was never a problem, and it had every kind of store you could think of, stocking the latest luxuries of the time.

But it wasn't to last. Everyone knew the story; one Monday morning in 1981, some kid's body had been found on the first-floor mezzanine.

A security guard was convicted of murdering the teenager, smashing the boy's face in with a blunt object, then fleeing the scene. If you listened to my mom, the case against him seemed a bit light, but a black guy on minimum wage night shift probably didn't get a very good lawyer. And nobody knew who the boy was; his teeth and jaw were pieced back together, but they didn't match any known dental records. In that typical, 1980s kind of way, everyone just tried to ignore that it had happened at first, to pretend that it was all erased by the guilty verdict.

I guess it was a different time. But then the store owners started reporting poltergeist activity; disembodied footsteps, whispers, stock moving by itself. When word got out that people were seeing ghosts, the popularity of the mall began to wane. Eventually, they shut up shop, store by store, until the mall was derelict, and in the summer of 1983, the doors were padlocked permanently shut.

Thirty years later, Tavistock Galleria still squatted beside the lake, too expensive to demolish, and too haunted to sell. Even the homeless folk avoided it, finding other places to hunker down for the night—there were plenty of other places without such dark histories.

"It's kind of a secret," Johnny told me, "can you keep a secret?"

I nodded fervently, "You know I can."

"All right. Sneak out tonight around 10:30, meet me by the mall. Bring a flashlight and your backpack—you'll need both."

"Ok."

We didn't talk about it anymore after that, absorbed as we were playing the new game Johnny bought. By the time I went home for dinner, I'd nearly forgotten the little prickle of fear I'd felt when he offered to show me the secret of Tavistock Galleria.

IT WAS a twenty-minute walk to the mall from my house, and I'd left late, because I'd had to wait for my dad to go to bed before I could sneak out. As soon as I got to the patch of weeds that had nearly reclaimed the cracked asphalt leading up to the mall, Johnny called out to me, his flashlight pointed down, a puddle of light at his feet.

"C'mon man, or we'll be late!"

I wondered how exactly we could be late for something that hadn't changed for three decades, but I hitched my empty backpack and hurried after him as he pushed through the tall grasses that grew high around the perimeter of the mall. The steel roller doors were still pulled down over the main entrance and sported rusted padlocks, but someone had kicked in the side of the corrugated metal, bending it in just enough for a person to climb through.

"This is how we get in," Johnny said, throwing his backpack through the hole, then clambering in after it.

I shelved my doubts and followed quickly, finding myself standing in a foyer littered with broken glass and drifts of dirty plastic sheeting.

"C'mon," Johnny called, his sneakers crunching across the glass as he led the way out into the mall concourse. Empty stores gaped, dark and cavernous, alarming shadows moving inside them as our flashlights swept past.

There was some sort of food court up ahead, or at least the remains of one. A few broken tables and plastic chairs were scattered about, flanked by tiled planters of overgrown ferns, forming a little indoor forest. Water pooled deep in one corner, and Johnny splashed through the shallows to reach the derelict escalator up to the first floor. His feet stirred up a green smell, rotting vegetation.

"Whole basement is flooded now," Johnny said as we climbed the ancient metal stairs, "Lake must've busted in and filled it all up. There's even fish in there, if you're brave enough to go down."

I shivered. I'd never been good with enclosed spaces or deep, dark water. I sure as shit wasn't going to go anywhere that combined both.

When we reach the mezzanine, he checked his watch, then flashed his teeth in a smile and nodded. "Right on time."

"What happens now?"

"Shh. Just listen and watch, OK? You'll see soon enough."

We stood in silence for a minute or so, my ears straining for the slightest hint of sound. At first, I could only hear the occasional drip of water below us, in the flooded section of the food court. But as I listened, another sound began to faintly intrude, drifting on the silence of the empty mall:

Old elevator music.

It was distant and eerie, tinny and thin, and distorted like it was echoing off objects that were no longer there. Chilly fear turned my throat sour, and the beam of my flashlight began to tremble, until Johnny put a steadying hand on my shoulder.

"It's OK, man. I've done this dozens of times. Chill."

Faint phosphorescence began to prick the corners of my vision and the music grew perceptibly louder, and more real. Between one blink and the next, I realized that the gaping storefronts around us were no longer empty sockets of darkness. Instead, a faint grey-white light dusted everything, showing us a sort of ghostly after-image of what had once been inside this place.

"Holy shit," I murmured.

Johnny laughed softly. "Yeah. Pretty fucking creepy, right? It always happens just after 11:11pm. Like clockwork."

Grabbing my arm, he hustled me along the cracked tiles of the mezzanine, making for the scratchy glow from one particular store.

"This one was Shirley's Candies." Squinting where Johnny pointed, I could see the eerie pale cursive of a neon sign scrawling itself across a window that didn't exist, spelling out its name. "My mom told me about it. She used to love the milkshakes from this place."

The music was louder here, real enough that my prickling ears could almost pinpoint the position of the invisible speakers it was coming from. Inside the candy store, the scratchy, faded white lines of shelves were superimposed over the rotten carpet and humps of broken, waterlogged ceiling tiles, like scrapes on the negative of a photograph.

"OK, so watch me," Johnny said, scanning the ethereal grid of ghostly shelves, "you gotta wait until the music sorta peaks. Then you can grab stuff."

His hand poised over one of the intangible shelves, we listened as the music ebbed and flowed. Suddenly, it surged and swelled, as though piped directly into our ears from another era.

Johnny swiped at shelves that now seemed less after-image, and more double-exposure—one reality layered over the top of another. With a whoop, he held up a very real box of Charleston Chews, and as the music faded away again, he stuffed the box into his backpack.

"You never know quite what you're gonna get," he told me, walking down the lattice of ghostly aisles, "but that's half the fun."

For the next two hours we moved from store to store, pilfering random goods from another time, until the music finally receded completely into the dark, replaced with the echoing silence of the abandoned mall.

I THOUGHT about the mall a lot over the next few days, wondering if what I'd experienced had been some weird fever-dream or hallucination. But the boxes of expired candy under my bed and the gleaming 'new' Atari 2600 beside my TV told a different story; one I was still struggling to believe. We went back again, nearly a week later, the unearthly, ancient music haunting us as our hands groped for forgotten treasures in those strange small hours when two different worlds seemed to cross over.

This time was easier at first. My lingering fear of the unknown had all but worn off, until Johnny suddenly grabbed my arm and pulled me down to the ground, hissing a warning.

"What?" I whispered, feeling my pulse ramp up as I crouched on the rotten linoleum.

Putting a finger to his lips, Johnny shook his head, then pointed through the smeared phosphorescence of the shelves in front of us. On the other side, a figure moved. Like the shelves, it was greyish-white and featureless, but certainly humanoid. And somehow deeply, deeply threatening.

My vision stuttered, my bladder clenched suddenly, and the urge to piss nearly overwhelmed me. As the creature moved toward us, Johnny kept his hand in a fistful of my hoodie sleeve, pulling me right through the insubstantial shelves and out onto the mezzanine, where he ducked into another shop. He looked like I felt, his eyes wild and his breath coming in ragged gasps.

"What the fuck was that?" I choked, my voice strangled in my throat. I'd never been so afraid in my life, and I had no idea why.

"Ghost," Johnny panted, "You gotta watch out for them. They come after you sometimes, chase you if they see you."

"Jesus fuck, Johnny! You never said shit about ghosts."

He spat into the darkness. "Well, it's a fucking haunted mall, isn't it? What the hell did you think would be here, Lewis? Why do you think everyone up and left in the first place?"

I swallowed my own sour saliva, not wanting to think too much about what had just happened.

"What do they do if they catch you?"

"I dunno, I've never been caught. Maybe they pull you into the ghost world. Maybe they steal your life to make themselves real. I'm not a fucking ghost expert, I just know, in my gut, that if they catch you something bad will happen. You felt that, right? You can feel the bad all around them, like death coming for you."

The music was fading away now; it was almost 1:11am, the time when the ghostly mall 'closed'. Heading for the foyer, I shook my head, shouldering my loot-filled backpack.

"Well in that case I'm not coming back here ever again. It's not worth it for some old candy and ancient video games."

Johnny said nothing as he climbed after me through the hole in the steel door. I wondered how many times he'd been here, and how many times he'd almost been caught. I wondered why he didn't just stop.

Worry ate at me every time Johnny turned up with a bag full of mall contraband to sell at school. He had an eBay account now, after buying his first laptop, and was starting to see some real profits from selling mint vintage goods to actual collectors. I tried to tell myself that he knew the risks, but the fact was he didn't know the risks. We had no idea what would happen if he got caught by the ghosts of Tavistock, and I felt like the world's shittiest friend for letting him put himself at risk like that. I'd always been Johnny's defender. Everyone knew it; that if they fucked with little scrawny Johnny Raisin, then Lewis Belmont, the tall, fast kid, would come and beat your ass for messing with his friend. Now he was facing something so much worse than kindergarten bullies, and even if he was doing it out of choice just because he wanted the money, I felt like crap for not being there for him when he needed me.

When Johnny turned up one day with a big bruise on the

side of his face and welt on his hand, I knew exactly what had happened.

"I fell," he tried to tell me.

"Like hell you did."

He gave me his lopsided grin and shrugged, "Well, they didn't catch me. I got away."

"Not without getting fucked up."

"I'm OK."

"You're not OK. You need to stop, Johnny."

His grin stuttered and faded, and I heard the receding mall music in my memory as his smile deserted him.

"I can't. I just... I can't, Lewis."

I blew out a long breath. "Fine. If you need to keep going back to that place, I'm coming with you. At the very least I can be your lookout, so the spooks don't get you."

I thought about how weird it was, that we were talking so casually about otherworldly spirits, as if they were just mall security that we needed to dodge while shoplifting.

"It was more fun with you there, anyway," Johnny said, forcing lightness back into his voice. I tried to do the same.

"Well, I guess that settles it then."

They seemed more vigilant now, the unnatural denizens of Tavistock Galleria—aware of us somehow; as though we'd been seen pilfering from their world and word had spread. I wondered if we'd outstayed our welcome, but Johnny was convinced everything was still OK. Whether that was just his greed talking or whatever else was driving him, I wasn't sure, but with my baseball bat tucked under my arm I felt less scared of the spirits that haunted this place.

I figured if they could hit Johnny, maybe I could hit them back.

We did all right for a while there, staying out of trouble. It was a big mall, and two hours seemed like a short enough time not to get caught. There had been a couple of close calls—Johnny couldn't run as fast as I could—but we knew the place well enough now that we could always find somewhere to hide.

Then it all came crashing down on us.

We'd been switching the days we went to the mall, as if it would confuse the ghosts, assuming they thought like we did. This time it was a Sunday. I'd been on guard at the top of the escalators when I heard pelting sneakers, then Johnny calling out to me, true alarm in his voice. Clutching one strap of his backpack, he was running as fast as he could along the top mezzanine, his stupid Michael Jackson jacket jingling as he ran. But the ghost was faster. It loped along behind him, all silvery-white limbs and rangy pale body, bearing down on him even as I ran to help, my baseball bat primed to swing.

And then it caught him, and everything turned red.

Blood spattered the mildewed tiles, bright at first, then darker and darker, as the ghostly thing smashed Johnny's head to a pulp. I remember every detail vividly; watching my friend's skull cave in with each impact from that blurry, grey-white arm, the limb too long, a streaky smear rising and falling. I felt like I was running through invisible barriers, distortions in the musty air, too slow. The bat swung hard in my hands, connecting with something solid, knocking the ghost away, and out of our world—but far too late. For just a moment, the wreckage of Johnny's ruined skull gaped up at me, all glistening brain and bright bone where my friend's face had been. Then he flickered out of existence, just as the mall music ebbed away.

Even as I raged and sobbed and paced, hunting up and down, waiting for the music to swell again, I already knew

Johnny was gone forever. There had always been something nagging at me about this place. It was more than just a ghost mall; the things we'd been stealing had been too real; too genuine and new. But that was a secondary concern. I knew that finding out her son was dead would quite literally be the end of Johnny's mom.

I got no sleep that night, nor the next. I begged off school with a migraine and sat on my computer, looking up anything I could about Tavistock Galleria and finding nothing. Eventually I emailed the local newspaper, asking if they had any of the old articles on file, and they obliged, sending me the original scanned article about the body. When I read the description of the battered corpse, all my fears were confirmed: Boy aged between 13-15 wearing a red jacket, a Laker's cap and new Levi jeans…

The original body that had started it all—the body that had cursed the mall in the first place—had been the body of my best friend, Johnny Raisin. We hadn't been stealing from a ghost mall at all. We were the ghosts, shoplifting goods from the past, making the people who owned the stores think the place was haunted.

I was so stupid, I should have been able to figure it out. Worst of all, I'd failed Johnny. I'd failed his mom too; and there was no fucking way I was ever going to tell her how he'd died.

The article contained the name of the security guard who had been charged with the murder of the unidentified boy, and I looked him up immediately. He'd been sentenced to life in a maximum-security prison, where he'd died several years later, killed by another inmate. The man had always protested his innocence, but I knew what had happened. I'd seen Johnny's death with my own eyes, and it was certainly murder.

But with the man dead already, there could be no justice for Johnny. No way I could pay him back for what he'd done. I eyed the baseball bat propped against my desk, remembering how solid Johnny's attacker had felt in that moment, how tangible the impact when I'd managed to knock him away.

Maybe there was a way to get payback after all?

WHILE THE POLICE hunted for Johnny Raisin, missing for a week now, I hunted for his killer.

Every night I went to the mall, waiting for the ghost. Sometimes I saw it, waving the pale smear of its long arm like it was taunting me, then it would vanish. Sometimes it ran from me and I'd give chase, ready to pay it back for all it had done to my friend. It was elusive; as if it knew I was hunting it. Sometimes it disappeared from one spot, then reappeared on the other side of the mall almost before it had faded from in front of me, almost as if there were two versions of it.

It became my mission, the focus for my grief. I managed to clip it with a pretty good swing one night, but it vanished again, and I stood and howled with rage, shaking my bat at the ceiling and swearing I would fucking kill the damn thing. And then it eventually happened, exactly as it should have.

I could tell the ghost had its back to me, and I ran, right as the music peaked, echoing through the abandoned mall. Hearing me, it turned, then fled along the mezzanine. Yelling incoherently, I chased it down, putting everything into my long strides—I was faster than it was—and as it stumbled, my bat came down on its head. Silver sparks exploded from it as it went down, and screaming with triumph, I struck it again and again, until brilliant silver pooled around what had been its skull. Too late, I saw another ghost approaching, charging straight for me, and then a powerful blow smashed straight into my jaw, knocking me sideways.

As I lay on the filthy floor, the world stuttered and flickered for a moment, like a slipped film.

And I saw red. A red jacket, a Laker's cap, a mangled skull; and an achingly familiar boy standing over us, holding a baseball bat.

~

It's been eight years since I murdered Johnny. Eight years since I discovered that there were never any 'ghosts' in that mall. Just echoes of ourselves, all tangled up in a big mess of temporal spaghetti, until none of it made sense anymore.

Johnny's mom died a year after his 'disappearance'. I arranged for her to be buried near the John Doe of Tavistock Galleria, so she could still be near her boy.

There's no way I can forgive myself for any of this, no way to atone for it. Tavistock Galleria still sits there, slowly rotting away, tempting me with its quantum mysteries, telling me I can go back and stop myself from killing Johnny, that I can fix everything.

But time doesn't work that way.

What's happened has happened, there can be no paradox, no change. Johnny's life was a perfect loop, and I was the hand that spliced it into shape.

Maybe one day I'll be rich enough to buy that time-forsaken mall and smash it into the dirt, but for now I still have too many demons to deal with.

Until then, I urge all of you: Just stay the fuck away from Tavistock Galleria.

# PROM DRESSES

PROM DRESSES

By Amanda Isenberg

THE FIRST TIME I HEARD ABOUT THE DRESS SHOP, I WAS IN THE back row of my best friend's minivan on the way to our favorite mall, Tavistock Galleria. It was 1995, and Jenny and I were sophomores in high school. Honestly, Jenny wasn't just my best friend, she was my only friend. We were not exactly popular. I was a bit overweight, and while that seemed to be fine for some girls, I was teased mercilessly for it. Likewise, Jenny was teased for her prominent crooked nose. I thought her nose made her look distinguished, but she couldn't wait until she grew up and could afford a nose job. Add our shared love of reading and our near perfect grades, and we were quite the outcast pair.

That particular trip to the mall was different. Jenny said she had a surprise for me. I begged her to give me a hint, but she refused.

"You'll see, Andrea," was all I could get out of her.

Jenny's dad dropped us off in front of the mall, reminding us to call when we were ready to be picked up.

"Do you have change for the pay phone?" he asked.

"Yes, Dad," Jenny replied. "Plus, I have my pager." She lifted the hem of her shirt enough to show the bright red pager sticking out of her pocket. I coveted that pager. My parents said I had to wait until I was 16 to get one.

"Ok. You girls have fun!" he called out as he rolled up the van window and pulled away.

"Jeez. He's so annoying!" Jenny said, rolling her eyes as we walked into the mall. I just snorted in reply. I didn't find Jenny's dad to be annoying at all. He really seemed to care about her. And he was always kind to me when he saw me. My own parents barely seemed to notice me.

We walked in silence for a while, passing the familiar stores. The Gap, which neither of us felt cool enough to shop at; Sam Goody, where we browsed for CDs while trying not to gawk at the cute sales staff; Claire's, where Jenny's mom had lied and said I was her daughter so I could get my ears pierced last year. My eyes darted around from stores to shoppers and back hoping to notice any of our crueler classmates before they noticed me. The mall was awash with spaghetti straps and flannel, and the scent of CK One permeated the air. At first, it seemed like Jenny was leading us toward our favorite store, Wet Seal.

"Jenny, this surprise better not be a sale at Wet Seal! You said it was good!" I had really been excited for the surprise, and I wasn't in the mood to be let down that day.

"Relax, Andrea! It will be good. I promise," she replied.

We walked past Wet Seal and soon found ourselves in a part of the mall we typically avoided. It was a short corridor off the main walkway. There wasn't much down there that I could remember. An off-brand cookie shop, a store that sold tacky jewelry and... that's it, I thought. But at the very end of the hall there was a new store. "Bess's Dresses" read the sign. Inside, the shop was filled with prom dresses. It was a sea of ruffles and lace and rhinestones and sequins. Jenny and I loved to try on prom dresses. It was the main reason we went to the mall, but we could do that at Macy's. Why would we need this place?

"Is this it?" I asked.

"Just wait," Jenny replied with a smile as she pulled me into the store.

The woman behind the counter was sewing sequins onto a hot pink gown. She had short dark hair and appeared to be middle aged. Behind her on the wall was a row of dresses that had been pressed and framed for display. She didn't look up from her sewing as we entered.

"Five dollars per dress," she called out to us. "Up front." Jenny started digging through her purse.

"What does she mean?" I whispered to Jenny.

"It's five bucks to try on a dress," she answered.

"Wait a minute!" I whispered to her. I grabbed her arm and drug her out of the store. "You want me to pay five dollars to try on a dress?! Jenny, first that's just dumb and second that's all I have for lunch!"

"Just trust me, ok? It's worth it. I promise. And I'll buy you lunch." Jenny smiled at me. "I wouldn't lie to you. You know that."

Reluctantly, I allowed myself to be led back into the store. I walked behind Jenny up to the counter where I deposited my crumpled five-dollar bill. The shop owner didn't even acknowledge us. She just glanced quickly at our cash and then returned to her sewing.

"Come on," Jenny said to me as she pulled me toward a rack in the rear of the store. "Let's find you the perfect dress."

"What about you?" I asked.

"I already have mine picked out," she replied.

Jenny began sorting through dresses, occasionally holding one up in my direction for a moment before changing her mind and slipping it back onto a rack. After a few minutes, I began doing the same. The entire situation seemed utterly bizarre to me, but I supposed that if I had paid five dollars to try on a dress, it better be worth it.

"This is it!" Jenny called out from a few aisles away. "This is your dress."

I walked over to her a looked slowly over the dress the held out to me. It was a gorgeous slinky silver slip dress. It was long and simple and perfect. And it would never fit me.

"Jenny…" I started. "That's beautiful. But it wouldn't fit half of me. Plus, my arms would show. You know I hate my arms."

"You are trying it on! You never know unless you try." Jenny sounded so sure that I didn't have it in me to argue.

It didn't occur to me to wonder where Jenny's dress was as we walked to the dressing room. The dressing area was small, just two stalls side by side with a large mirror adjacent to their doors. Hanging on the back of one of the doors was a flowy seafoam green dress.

"That one is mine," Jenny said proudly.

"Wait, it was just waiting for you? What the hell?"

Jenny sighed. "The owner probably snuck back here and hung it up. I've been here before. Duh. How do you think I know about this place? Anyway, don't act so freaked out. Come on. Try on your dress."

Jenny thrust the dress at me and I took it, then turned and

walked into the stall. I made sure I locked the door behind me then began to take off my clothes. I was careful not to look at myself in the mirror as I undressed. I hated so much about my body. My thick, frizzy hair, my large breasts and thighs, my soft stomach. I was pretty much the antithesis of Kate Moss. I unzipped the dress and slid it over my head. To my surprise, it fell to my ankles instead of catching at my hips as I thought it would. I reached around awkwardly and tugged the zipper up. Looking down, I saw that the dress was snug from my chest to my hips instead of draping loosely as it was meant to. I didn't bother turning to look in the mirror.

"Ready?" Jenny called out.

"I guess," I replied sullenly.

"Don't sound so excited! Come on out."

Slowly, I unlocked the door and stepped out. The dressing room door slammed behind me, and I found myself staring at a row of sinks and mirrors. I was in a bathroom. Suddenly, Jenny grabbed my arm.

"You look amazing!" she squealed.

"Jenny, what the hell is going on?! Where are we? What the hell. What the hell." I was practically shrieking at her. This was not the mall. I had no idea where this was.

"Calm down, Andrea. It's ok. I promise. Come here." Jenny spoke in soothing tones as she pulled me to a large mirror. "Look at yourself. Just look."

"Jenny, where the hell are we?!" I yelled.

"Andrea! Look!" She pointed at the mirror. I let my eyes move to the wall in front of me. What I saw caused my mouth to fall open. I looked like a different person. My face was mostly the same, only leaner, but everything else was changed. I was at least twenty pounds lighter. The slip dress hung delicately off my shoulders and fell gracefully to the floor. My hair was long and straight. I turned to look at Andrea. She looked elegant in her gown. Her hair fell down her back in loose curls. And something else was different. It was her face.

"Oh my god," I gasped. "Your nose!"

"I know, right? Can you believe it?" She turned to look at herself in the mirror. Her nose was perfect. It was an adorable, tiny button nose.

"Okay, you were right. This is totally worth five dollars. How is all of this even possible?" I asked her.

"You haven't seen the best part," she replied as she began pulling me toward the bathroom door. "Now you have to promise me you won't freak out. You have to play it cool."

"Play it cool for what?" I asked.

"Promise me, Andrea. Pinky swear." She thrust her pinky at me.

"What am I promising?" I asked, but Jenny just glared at me in reply. "Okay, okay! I pinky swear." I hooked my pinky around hers.

"Great," she replied. "Let's go." She pulled the bathroom door open and we walked out. The room was dimly lit, but it was obviously huge. Music blared around us, and lights bounced around what appeared to be a dance floor. Glittering stars hung from the ceiling, and white clothed tables ringed the room. Hundreds of people moved around the room decked out in tuxedos and gowns. I heard laughter and talking beneath the booming music.

"Jenny," I whispered. "Is this...prom?"

She shushed me. Two guys in tuxedos approached us.

"There you girls are. We were looking for you," one of them said to us. It took me a moment to register who they were. It was Chad and Chris, our long-time crushes.

"We were just in the bathroom," Jenny laughed in reply. "Andrea had to fix her lipstick."

"You look beautiful, babe," Chad said to me as he reached for my hand. I let him take it, too stunned to speak. "Let's dance?" he asked.

After an awkward moment, I was able to nod a reply. He pulled me to the dance-floor as The Smashing Pumpkins' song "Tonight, Tonight" began. Chad stood in front of me and placed his hands on my waist. For a moment, I stood there and did nothing.

"Babe?" he said, a concerned look on his face. I reached up and placed my arms around his neck.

"Sorry," I managed to mumble.

I was too confused and shocked to look at Chad for more than a second at a time. I noticed his wavy hair that hung just past his ears. I was close enough to smell his cologne, and I caught a whiff of mint on his breath. Mostly, my eyes darted around the room trying to take in everything that was happening around me. The lights and movement began to blur, and dizziness washed over me. The song ended, and I pulled away. "I need to find Jenny," I said.

"But you just saw her," Chad called after me as I rushed away. Luckily, I found Jenny quickly. She had her back to a wall, and Chris was leaning over her whispering something into her ear. She laughed softly and reached out to rest her hand on his shoulder.

"Jenny!" I called out. "I need to talk to you. Now!"

Jenny looked startled, but she stepped away from Chris. "What is it?" she asked.

"You know what," I replied. "Come with me."

I pulled her back into the bathroom. "Look," I began. "I

don't know what is going on here, but I am really freaking out. I want to go."

"But we just got here," she answered. I cut her off before she could say anything else.

"I need to go. Now. Please." Tears welled up in my eyes and began to fall down my cheeks.

"Oh, sweetie, okay. Of course we can go. Come on. Just go inside the bathroom stall, turn around and walk back out. Let's go." Jenny patted my arm sympathetically.

I did exactly as she said and found myself back in the dressing room at the mall. I quickly changed out of the dress. When I turned toward the mirror, I saw that I looked like myself again for better or worse. Jenny and I left the store, and she called her dad to come pick us up. We didn't speak about the dresses or the store until later when we were alone in Jenny's bedroom.

"Jenny, what was that place?" I began hesitantly. I was still in shock from the experience and a bit afraid to ask about exactly what happened. "How did you find it?"

Jenny took a deep breath. "It freaked me out, too, the first time. It was a week ago. I was at the mall by myself. I'd never been down that hall before, but when I saw the store, it called to me. I can't really explain it. The owner was standing near the front and she called me in asking if I wanted to try on a dress. She didn't charge me, didn't tell me anything about what would happen. I tried on a dress and, well, you saw what happens next. I was so confused. Scared even. But when I went out and saw the dance… I stayed. It was so amazing."

"How many times have you done it now?" I asked hesitantly.

"Today was my third time. Andrea, wasn't it amazing? When you calm down and think about it, it's perfect, right? I mean, we are beautiful, and Chad and Chris are there and they like us. Ok, so I didn't know that Chad would be there when you came, but I had a hunch and I was right!" Jenny was speaking rapidly. Her excitement was contagious.

"I suppose it was pretty cool," I reluctantly agreed.

"So, you want to go back?! I can't wait! It gets better the longer you stay." Jenny grabbed my hands and gave them a squeeze.

"Okay, okay. We can go back," I replied hoping my voice didn't betray my nervousness.

The next day Jenny convinced her dad to take us to the mall again. She paid the five dollars for each of us, and we tried on the dresses. This time, my dress was already hanging in the dressing room, waiting for me. We took a moment to look ourselves over in the bathroom mirror before walking into the dance.

"There you girls are. We were looking for you," Chris said as we stepped away from the bathroom. Jenny laughed in reply.

"You look beautiful, babe," Chad said to me reaching for my hand. "Let's dance?"

"Of course," I replied.

I was amazed by how much more confident I felt this time. I took Chad's hand and let him lead me to the dance floor. I draped my arms around his neck and leaned into him as we swayed to the Smashing Pumpkins.

The evening passed in a blur. We danced, we sat at a large table surrounded by friends and laughed. I had my first kiss to Mazzy Star's "Fade into You." Eventually, Jenny whispered in my ear that it was time to go. Reluctantly, I excused myself to the bathroom again. When Jenny and I found ourselves back in the dressing room, I checked my watch to find that three hours had passed. Jenny saw me staring at my watch.

"Time passes the same there as it does here," she told me. I barely listened to her. I was glowing. I had just spent the most amazing three hours of my life. Jenny linked her arm into mine and we left the store, both of us smiling like fools. The store owner didn't even glance up at us. Like before, her attention was on the gown she was sewing.

The dresses and prom became all Jenny and I talked about. We used every excuse we could to get back to the mall. I found myself blushing uncontrollably when I passed Chad in the hall at school. After a couple weeks, I noticed Jenny had stopped eating. Soon after, my appetite disappeared as well. Jenny had always been thin, but now she was beginning to look skeletal. Jenny's parents stared at her worriedly as she pushed food around her plate. She always promised them she would eat at the mall, so they gave her more and more money hoping what she said was true.

During one visit to prom, we discovered that a friend of a friend had a flask of cheap whiskey. After that, we spent part of each visit getting tipsy then spinning around the dance floor laughing and hanging on each other. For me, the alcohol made everything blurry around the edges and somehow more beautiful. I felt bolder and more alive. On one visit, I asked Chad if he wanted to go to his car for a while. I wasn't sure if we'd be able to leave the building, but we were. I lost my virginity that night in the backseat of his car, the street lights peeking in and out of branches and creating dancing shadows in the car. It was magical.

In real life, Jenny's grades were slipping, and she continued to grow thinner and thinner. Our classmates began to whisper about her when she passed by. I heard words like "anorexia" tossed around. I was losing weight too, but my parents just complimented me for finally starting to thin out. Jenny grew quieter, even when it was just the two of us alone in her bedroom. She slipped into long, distracted silences that I was unable to snap her out of.

One day at school she walked up to Chris and said, "Hey babe."

At first, he looked shocked, but then he burst out laughing.

"What the hell is this?" he managed to get out between laughs.

I grabbed Jenny's arm and pulled her away. When I looked back, Chris was still laughing. Chad was standing next to him. He looked at me with a smile and winked.

The last time we went to prom was on a Saturday night. Jenny didn't speak during the drive. I could see her father's worried eyes glancing at her in the rearview mirror. I held her hand as we walked to the dress shop. Her fingers were cold and blue. I had read that this was due to poor circulation caused by not eating for so long. Outside the dressing room door, I gave her a hug. She smiled at me, the first smile I had seen from her in a long time. We went in, and suddenly were back in our dream world. Jenny was healthy at prom. She smiled and laughed and talked with me.

It was a beautiful night. We drank and danced and laughed with our friends. I asked Chad to take me to his car, and we made love again. At the end of the night, I had to practically drag Jenny back to the bathroom. The last thing she said to me before we went into the stalls was, "I'm so happy here. It's everything I ever wanted." Then she was gone.

I changed back into my clothes and opened the dressing stall door. I waited a few moments for Jenny to come out, then called her name. Nothing. I knocked on the stall door.

Still nothing. Finally, I opened it to find it empty. No dress, no clothes, no Jenny. I ran to the front of the store.

"Have you seen my friend? Did she already leave?" I asked the woman behind the counter.

"What friend?" she replied, not looking up from her sewing. "You came in alone."

"No, I came in with my friend. The same friend I always come in with." I protested.

"Time to leave. I'm closing up." She looked up at me. Her eyes were cold and threatening.

"But..." I tried but was interrupted.

"Leave before I call security."

I backed slowly out of the store. The woman immediately pulled down the security gate. I ran to a pay phone and called Jenny's house. Her dad answered.

"Jenny is missing!" I blurted out. "We were trying on dresses and she just disappeared. Please, I can't find her."

"Andrea, calm down. I'll be right there." He sounded calm and collected.

I sank down to the floor under the pay phone and pulled my knees to my chest. Twenty minutes later, Jenny's dad found me there. I took him to the dress shop and he peered in. He managed to get mall security involved, and soon they called the police. While they were talking to Jenny's dad, I looked in through the gate and into the store. That's when I saw it. Behind the counter, framed on the wall beside a row of other dresses was Jenny's dress. I began to scream.

The rest of the night passed in a blur. I tried again and again to explain about the dresses, the store, the prom. No one listened. No one believed me. Eventually the police drove me home. They explained what happened to my parents, but I didn't listen. I just climbed the stairs to my room and fell into my bed. No one checked on me that night.

Weeks passed. Fliers with Jenny's face were plastered around town. At first, there were search parties combing the nearby woods. Soon, people gave up on searching. The fliers began to tear and fall off the bulletin boards and telephone poles. No one replaced them.

I became the girl with the missing friend. People were kind to me. They hugged me in the school halls and asked how I was feeling. They complimented how thin I was becoming. I didn't care. I was numb. A dull pain the size of a fist formed in my stomach. It became the only thing I could feel. Eating eased the pain, so I didn't eat. Even after people seemed to forget about Jenny, they still paid attention to me. They seemed to mistake my apathy and distance for attitude and mystery. Suddenly, I was cool.

My path eventually crossed Chad's, and he became interested in me. We began dating. He didn't seem to mind that I had nothing to say so long as he could walk through the halls with his arm draped over my shoulders. We had sex in the backseat of his car, and it wasn't at all like I remembered. I felt nothing save an initial sharp pain. I stared silently out the rear window of the car and up at the full moon.

I learned that Chad's older brother would get us alcohol if Chad asked. And Chad was more willing to ask if we had sex. I spent most of my time drinking and screwing on the worn-out sofa in Chad's basement. Being drunk helped me forget about Jenny for a while.

More than a year had passed since I last saw Jenny. I was a junior. I agreed to go to prom with Chad. My mom actually drove me to the mall to look for dresses. I had become thin enough that my parents took notice and had begun to worry.

My hair had been thinning for a while. My brush was constantly full of hair no matter how often I cleaned it. My fingers turned blue often. That made me feel closer to Jenny.

I tried on dresses at Macy's, my mom waiting outside the dressing room door. I slipped the first one on and turned to look in the mirror. My hair fell thin and straight past my shoulders. The dress hung from my reedy frame. I was the girl I had seen so many times in the bathroom mirror with Jenny. I had become who I always wanted so badly to be. I felt hot rage flow through my body. I hated what happened to Jenny, I hated what happened to me. I began to scream an angry, guttural shriek as a punched my image in the mirror. I hit it again and again, even after it cracked and splintered, even after blood began streaming from my split knuckles.

My mother burst in the dressing room trying to restrain me. Store employees and security guards soon followed. I don't remember much else until I woke up in the emergency room with a cast on my hand. I was still wearing the dress. Later, my mother went back to Macy's and purchased the dress. She even managed to clean the blood out. Chad and our friends thought I was "badass" for punching a mirror and breaking my hand. They had no idea about the real story, and I didn't tell them anything.

I saw Jenny one last time. It was at prom. I'd walked through the doors at the start of the evening and stopped short. It was exactly the same as the prom Jenny and I had attended so many times.

"Babe?" Chad inquired, his eyebrows raised. I laughed grimly to myself then took his outstretched arm and kept walking.

The evening felt so hollow, so empty. I danced with Chad to the same songs but felt nothing. I was drunk halfway through the night. Too drunk. I stumbled to the bathroom feeling sick. I managed to lean over a toilet just in time to vomit. I laughed to myself that if Jenny would have been there, she'd be holding my hair. If Jenny would have been there, none of this would be happening.

Wiping my mouth with the back of my good hand, I stumbled to a sink to wash my face. As I looked up into the mirror, I saw her. She was reflected in the adjacent mirror, the one we had admired ourselves in so many times. Slowly, I crossed to the mirror. She was wearing the dress. She was looking right at me. Her body was fragmented, like she was made of broken glass. I could see through her. She didn't speak or move, just stood there staring at me. After a moment, I broke her gaze and walked out of the bathroom and back to the dance.

Nowadays Tavistock Galleria is a shadow of its former self. I go back now and again. I walk past the empty stores along the path Jenny and I took so many times. The dress shop never reopened. I can peer into it through the security gate. The rows of racks that once held countless dresses are empty. But above the front counter, the framed dresses remain. Jenny's dress is still there. It's perfect, untouched by time. I stare at it, trying to remember Jenny wearing it, trying to see her one more time, but I never can. In the end, all I can do is let out the breath I didn't know I was holding and turn and walk away.

# TAVISTOCK AFTER DARK

# TAVISTOCK AFTER DARK

By L.P. Hernandez

"Now that you've seen our faces we can never let you leave," the old man said, tightening his grip on Joe's shoulder

The implication and the words not spoken were evident.

*I won't tell anyone.*

The sentence bubbled in Joe's throat but failed to coalesce.

There was nothing to be said. There was nothing to be done.

"I can't promise it will be painless. But it will be efficient."

The old man smiled, revealing white gums and a row of teeth the color of cinder blocks. The attendees nodded in unison.

It was not a series of poor decisions that lead to Joe's temporary employment at the mall. It was the absence of decisions all together.

He labored through college to secure a meaningless degree that delivered him right back to his childhood bedroom. Somewhere along the way *getting back on my feet* became a permanent lifestyle choice.

Joe woke one morning to find the classified section of the newspaper taped to his television. The Tavistock Galleria position was circled in red with the words *Call them. Do it!* scribed next to it.

That is how Joe found himself stalking through the mostly abandoned mall long after the last patron had left. From 11 PM until sunrise he was the sole occupant, his echoing footfalls serenaded by warbling muzak. His job was to inventory and document the condition of *Real Property.*

"If you turned the mall upside down and gave it a good shake, whatever didn't come loose is real property," he'd been told.

Joe was to document obvious defects: cracks, peeled paint, carved initials, et cetera. It was a two-week job that paid $15 an hour.

There were other benefits as well. He realized on his second night of work that the Chinese restaurant in the food court did not turn off the soda fountain at night. An added bonus.

Joe walked toward the food court just before midnight leading into Thursday morning. He hummed along to a neutered rendition of "November Rain." Although he detested muzak in general, he preferred it to the alternative, which was silence. The brief interlude between songs was unsettling, like the stillness in the aftermath of a massacre.

Joe stood at the soda fountain and hummed to "November Rain's" saxophone solo. He topped off his 48 oz Thermos with one last splash of Dr Pepper while taking in the surroundings which seemed so familiar yet artificial, as if it was a movie set. He could almost hear the voices of his friends as they dashed toward the arcade in his memory. He'd spent hours in that arcade, chasing tickets to buy some novelty toy he could have purchased for cash at one-tenth the cost. Hot Topic carried him from his emo phase into his hardcore metal phase. He mowed seven lawns in one weekend to save up enough money to buy his first girlfriend perfume from the Dillard's at the opposite end of the mall.

The mall was more than just a place to spend money. It was a place of joy, and now he was surveying its bones and documenting their potential value.

"November Rain" ended and Joe cocked his head to the side. He scratched a peanut butter-brown beard that was no longer a fashion choice. The voices from his memory persisted, muted but close. That was strange. Joe walked toward the faint sound, sipping his soda as "Africa" by Toto flooded the empty space.

Although he no longer heard the voices he continued in the direction from which they originated. There was a Claire's to his right; impossibly one of the few stores still operating as the mall prepared to close its doors. It seemed silly, but part of him mourned for the loss of these cultural touchstones. Did middle school girls still make a day of getting their ears pierced at Claire's?

It was not talking. It was singing. He guessed a radio was errantly left on in one of the stores. Not worth exploring.

Except...

There was something odd about the singing. It reminded him of those chanting monk CDs that had been popular in the 90s.

Joe stood in front of the Radio Shack, which had been

among the first stores to close. The chanting was definitely coming from within the store, which had not hosted a customer in more than a year.

The inside was hidden behind aluminum shutters, but Joe could access it from the employee entrance.

"Gonna take a lot to drag me away from you..." he sang as he walked.

His stride lengthened as he entered the hallway that led to the backside of the store. He walked through a set of heavy-duty swinging doors into what had been Radio Shack's storeroom. He flipped the light switch several times before abandoning the effort in favor of his cell phone flashlight.

"What the..."

There were shoes and other clothing items neatly arranged along the wall. Luxury brand purses hung from brass hooks formerly used by Radio Shack employees. There was no overhead speaker in this room and the sound of chanting was both incredibly clear and close.

Joe shifted his weight from one foot to the other, the soda in his empty belly sloshing uncomfortably. There was no reason to go any further. The chanting subsided in favor of an unintelligible orator. The voice was a thrumming baritone with a watery texture. Joe inched forward, approaching a door that would lead him into the store.

Maybe he could just peek...

The speaker's words were repeated back to him as Joe cracked the door. What he saw did not make sense. The room was illuminated by candlelight. Curtains of red velvet adorned the walls. Thirty or more hooded people stood with their backs to Joe. They were as still as tombstones and facing the same direction.

All except one.

At the far end of the store, what used to be a store, a figure sat behind an altar. Before the altar was a basin whose contents, mostly obscured by dancing shadows, glistened wetly in the candlelight. Joe's gaze alternated between the vivisected woman on the altar and the figure seated behind her. He, presumably he, wore a silken robe, ink black and trimmed with vermillion. A goat's head rested atop his shoulders, a crown of black thorns encircling its stunted horns.

The figure held a golden staff, its intricate details not discernible from where Joe stood. He slammed the staff on the floor and the mass spoke words in a tongue Joe had never before heard. It was a brutish language of harsh and guttural words, the sounds of a condemned, hanging from a noose. The staff connected with the floor again and the mass took their seats.

"Don't go roaming the halls at night. As tempting as it might be, we're not paying you to explore. Plus, some shops still have inventory. If anything goes missing they'll look to you first." Steve, the man who hired him, had said.

"Of course," Joe replied, recoiling from the old man's breath, which smelled like a sneaker that had been left to molder in the rain.

Had there been more to the warning?

Unused adrenaline turned Joe's muscles into bricks. The room was silent. He weighed his options for escape and feared even a stray squeak of his shoes would alert them to his presence. As soon as the chanting began again he would ease out of the room, creep back into the hallway, and make a mad dash for the parking lot.

The figure behind the altar stood. It was so quiet Joe could hear the muzak version of Paula Abdul's "Straight Up" playing in the mall. He lifted one arm robotically and aimed a gloved figure at the back of the room. Hot breath tickled the back of Joe's neck. Thirty faces turned to watch as he was ushered into the room. In the flickering candlelight Joe saw at least one he recognized, his high school principal. There were likely others, but his vision had narrowed to a pinpoint.

His legs wilted, but he was caught before he fell.

"It was a simple request, wasn't it Joe? Do your job and don't go exploring."

He vomited hot Dr. Pepper from the wretched stench of the old man's breath and was allowed to fall to the floor. His consciousness faded.

*Lost in a dream,*
*I don't know which way to go...*

# MALL WALKERS

## MALL WALKERS

By A.J. Horvath

"Three years...has it really been three years?" I thought to myself as I stared at the cheesy *You're the Bee's Knees* dollar store card my boss had given me with a stale cupcake. Time flies I guess. I began working at the Tavistock Galleria when I was 16. My dad said it would build character, plus he refused to pay for my gas and phone any longer. I didn't really mind too much; it wasn't really hard work. I stocked shelves, helped customers, cleaned up after everyone, and ultimately tried not to die of boredom.

You come to find that there are certain categories of shoppers and you just need to identify and accommodate as that person's category requires. You always have the moms who are tired and snippy. Take care of them quickly and don't give their kids (who will probably mess up half your inventory) a sideways glance and you are golden. You have the browsers who want to be left alone and the serious shoppers who ask way too many ridiculous questions and wonder why you, an employee in a mall store, don't understand the molecular structure of the item you're trying to sell.

Then, after all that, you have the typical teenage mall goer. There are several sub-types of teens; different manners of dress, hair style, you name it, but most of them just walk around not buying anything because they are broke. Some of them have sticky fingers and you have to keep an eye out, but at my store that really isn't an issue. We maybe get like three customers a day. Seriously. I have no idea how we stay in business, but we do.

My boss and the owner of the store was Mr. Ulkovich. He was stern, quick to anger, and barely around. I saw him weekly to get my schedule and my check but otherwise I had no idea where he was. I split the shifts with two other teenager who went to my school, but we ran in different cliques, so we didn't really communicate outside of work. I spent most of my shifts just watching people walk by the store. I was always making up stories about what they were here for, what their life was like outside the mall. It was silly, really, but it helped pass the time.

My favorites were the mall walkers. We had a group of six really avid ones. All of them were at least seventy and without fail, every day when the mall opened at 10 am they were there making their rounds. There were Doris and Mable, twins who had lived in town their whole lives. Then there was Mr. and Mrs. Jensen, happily married for 55 blissful years. Mr. Selbman was a crotchety old man who came along just to complain as far as I could tell—something was always aching, the teens didn't know anything, and the government was taking all his money. My favorite by far though was Mr. Clemmons, who always told me to call him Jimmy. He was a funny old guy, a veteran from the Marines, and he always had a story or two to tell me; life lesson as he liked to call them. We usually met up in the food court on my lunch break and played a game of travel chess.

Things had been going as they typically do, a few random people came in, shifted around our items and left without purchasing anything. I quickly cleaned up the mess and checked my watch: 11:25. Looking out the shop entrance, I watched the group of mall walkers come around the bend making their way towards the shop. Jimmy beamed at me, jerking a thumb over at the twins and signaling to stay clear. I had to laugh. Jimmy was a riot and those twins were in a feud over something every other week. When they finally made it to the shop entrance it was 11:28 and I yelled to my co-worker Brandon that I was leaving a couple minutes early for my lunch break. He didn't even bring his eyes up from his phone as he muttered his consent.

Setting up the chess board, Jimmy told me that since shoplifting had been on the rise, Tavistock was launching a new program and that he and the other walkers were going to be a part of it. I had heard other mall workers talking about it during breaks and in the parking lot after shifts. The new program would take those who shoplifted and make them walk with the seniors while picking up trash and learning from a good mentor. I had to admit it wasn't a bad idea. Plus, these old folks loved a chance to talk someone's ear off. Though, I felt sorry in advance for the poor kid who got stuck with cranky Mr. Selbman.

Jimmy also informed me that a guy from another mall that already used this program was coming to get this one up and running. Wilfred Chronister, as far as Jimmy knew, was a strict old gentleman in his mid-80s; however, there was something that Jimmy couldn't quite put his finger on. Something about him felt off, something behind his eyes. Jimmy didn't really elaborate further but he did a good job kicking my ass in chess, as usual.

The next week I watched as the normal group of walkers made their rounds joined by three new faces. The teenagers plodded along, dejected eyes to the ground, as they followed their elderly counterparts. Jimmy walked over beaming at me. He was thrilled to have these kids around. We took our places at our table, but this time the others were there too, sitting near us in the surrounding tables. The twins were with a blonde girl who sat looking bored whilst twirling her long hair around a perfectly manicured finger. The lovebirds had a young Hispanic guy, dressed in all black; his eyes obscured by the bangs he kept over his brow. Mr. Selbman sat with a large guy; his stomach poking out under his ill-fitting sweatshirt. His curly hair clung to his forehead where the sweat seemed to never stop flowing.

Jimmy told me all he knew about the trio and their supposed infractions: The big one stole candy from a center shop, the blonde lifted some lingerie, and the Hispanic boy took some skateboard accessories. He didn't have one assigned to him yet, but Mr. Chronister promised him that he would get the next offender that came into the program. Our game went fast and, of course, Jimmy won.

The next week it was still the same three kids, but they seemed to have changed somehow. They seemed bone tired, drained almost. I had to do a double take to even recognize them. The walkers looked happier than ever, a bit of pep in their step and even Mr. Selbman had a hint of what might be called a smile on his lips. Jimmy looked a bit dejected and told me he didn't feel up for lunch or chess, which was odd, but I wasn't going to push.

The weeks passed, and the group changed significantly. The walkers seemed cheerier, less prone to stopping or hobbling along as they once had. Mr. Selbman was definitely smiling now even though his large companion had stopped coming to the offender program. However, for some reason Jimmy kept his distance from me, which hurt, but I wasn't going to pry.

One day, I was headed off for lunch and was suddenly pulled into a storefront. Jimmy grasped at my arm, wildly stating that I had to get out and that the young people were in danger. Mr. Chronister was doing something unnatural. Evil. It was then his eyes grew wide with fear and a shadow overtook us both. I turned to see who I assumed was Mr. Chronister.

He was stern looking man with a severe nose and beady, bird-like eyes. His dark mustache was neatly trimmed, and his dark hair edged in grey was coiffed appropriately for a man his age. He said hello and walked a few steps away before signaling for Jimmy to join the group again.

I felt sorry for him. Mr. Chronister seemed like a real pain the ass, but evil things? This just had to be an elaborate prank. Jimmy was known to do that every now and then. The twins didn't talk to him for a month for the whoopie cushion he'd brought in a few months before. I decided I would see for myself what this Chronister guy was really like. I didn't work the next day, so I decided to do some reconnaissance.

I followed the group, but not too closely as to avoid suspicion. I knew their route well from having worked here for so long, except towards the end, they didn't stop at the center station but continued down towards the store that had been closed for renovation. Chronister led the group to a storefront that had a large

"Coming Soon" banner slapped across the windows, the rest of the clear glass covered in a brown paper wrapping for suspense. I hurried over to the door and cracked it open.

The walkers sat in a semi-circle with Mr. Chronister looming in front of them. On the floor was the blonde girl... or what *used* to be the blonde girl. She lay in a shriveled heap, barely moving. Mr. Chronister stood over her, eyes closed and lips moving as if speaking but I could hear nothing. Around his neck was an amulet that he gripped tightly in his hand. A soft blue glow emanated from his fist.

I gasped as the girl's body began to levitate. The noise attracted the attention of the walkers who turned quickly in unison. Their eyes locked on me and my body went into fight or flight mode. I stumbled backwards, falling hard on my ass and trying in a panicked scramble to get back on my feet and run. I could hear the heavy footfalls of the walkers behind me as I rounded corners trying to escape. At last I found a store that was quite busy and dashed inside. I tried to be as quiet as possible while catching my breath. The old group rushed by, no hint of old age in their movements. I had no idea what was going on, but it had to be something to do with whatever Chronister had in his hand.

It was probably stupid, but I had to go back and save that poor girl. I snuck back through the mall, only seeing the walkers a couple of times as they continued to hunt for me. As quietly as was manageable, I slowly opened the door once more. The girl still lay on the floor, but the room was otherwise empty. I made my way to her still body and checked for a pulse, but before I could find one, a scuffle and squeaking sneakers caught my attention. Chronister stood a few feet away, holding Jimmy tightly, the old man wincing in pain as his arm was wrenched behind his back. I stopped and slowly rose from the girl's side.

"Well, it has come to this," Mr. Chronister said ominously. "It isn't common for us to be found out so quickly...or at all for that matter. You see, this is a matter of survival dear child and I have been surviving for many, many years."

"What do you mean? You are a complete nut!" I yelled at him, hearing Jimmy groan as Mr. Chronister pulled his arm fiercely.

"A nut you say? Would a nut know the ways of everlasting life? Would a nut be someone who has avoided detection and capture for this long? If so, I guess I am as nutty as they come. Your life force is strong and good little Jimmy here was tasked with delivering you to me. However, you seem to have pulled his little heartstrings and he disobeyed so I had to improvise," he smiled devilishly.

Jimmy's eyes locked on mine and I watched him mouth a silent countdown...3...2...1. He moved quickly, stomping his orthopedic shoe square onto Mr. Chronister's immaculate leather wingtip. Chronister screamed in agony and then in rage as he realized that in the scuffle, Jimmy had ripped the amulet from his neck and thrown it to me. He growled at Jimmy, throwing him roughly to the ground. I heard the snapping of bones and knew that Jimmy was seriously hurt as he groaned and writhed on the ground.

"You pathetic waste of life!" Mr. Chronister spat, his eyes emanating hatred as he stared down at the heap that was Jimmy. I held the amulet tightly in my fist. It was a clear crystal affixed to a gold necklace. The crystal was carved with strange symbols and small pictures. I held the amulet high above my head to catch the attention of Mr. Chronister. His eyes grew wide as he saw what I planned to do and dove forward with all his might. The crystal smashed on the ground, splintering into tiny pieces. Mr. Chronister's face contorted and as his body hit the ground, it cracked and burst into a cloud of fine gray dust. I stood in shock, staring at the pile of dust that was once Mr. Chronister. Jimmy's groans pulled me out of my awe and I ran to his side.

The rest was a blur. I called security and an ambulance came for both Jimmy and the blonde girl. Jimmy had suffered a broken shoulder and hip but would otherwise be ok. The blonde girl was hospitalized and seemed to be catatonic. Her parents later put her in an institution for further psychiatric care. The police questioned me and the other walkers but we all knew better than to tell the truth. We would be put away for being crazy.

After speaking with Jimmy, I did some research on the other malls that Mr. Chronister had been a part of. I found a trail of missing children reports and a slew of obituaries of members of the walking groups that had been a part of Chronister's program. Twenty lives as far as I could tell but who knows how many more that man had taken all in a vain attempt for eternal life.

As time went on, the walkers all stopped coming in as they began to age in an expedited fashion. The twins were the first to go, their funeral was short and ill-attended. Mr. Selbman was next, and then finally the married couple who died within hours of each other. Whatever they had stolen from their teenage charges with Chronister's magic was now repaid in full.

# THE FOUNTAIN

# THE FOUNTAIN

By Desdymona Howard

WHEN I WAS LITTLE MY GRANDMOTHER KEPT ME A LOT DURING the summer. My mom was a single parent and she had to work, so she'd drop me off with Grams and we'd hang out all day. She wasn't so old she couldn't keep up with me, but she was retired and that left her the ability to keep me. We always enjoyed each other's company and she would let me "veg out" in the living room and play videos games for hours on end.

That summer, Grams and her old lady friends were on an exercise kick. We went to the park to walk the trails, which I enjoyed. And they tried some weird exercise videos which would force me to hide. That was a traumatizing sight if I ever saw one. On the first day I tried to join in. Seemed like a good idea; might even be fun. That was until we started stretching and Gale who didn't realize she had moved too close to me bent over to stretch, and BAM old lady butt hit me in the face. After that, I would read a book on the front porch or play in the backyard in order to save my retinas and dignity. While getting a soda from the fridge one day, I overheard Gale suggest that they go power walk at the mall.

"I was shopping for a gift for Dean for his birthday and I stopped by the Tavistock Galleria. That place is really declining, but I think it'd be a better place to take our walks than in the the park. We'll be inside with the air conditioning. No sun burns and no heat!"

The others agreed. "Oh, what a fantastic idea, Gale! We could do some shopping too!"

And Linda, the cynical one, who probably had 15 years on them all but was spunky as all get out chimed in. "Are you sure there aren't any hooligans to mess with us? I ain't dealing with any delinquents Abigail Elise Martin!"

Gale assured them that the Tavistock Galleria was all but dead and that she had not seen any delinquents at all on her recent visit "Not even by that Hot Pocket store upstairs."

"Oh darling, those stores invite delinquents, my neighbor's kid works at one of those and he wears the most awful outfits and smokes cigarettes in their backyard. Makes me gag every time I water my flowers. I don't want to run into his type when we are walking," retorted Linda.

The very next day right after my mom dropped me off, Grams loaded us into the car and we headed off to the mall. I bounced in the passenger seat all the way there.

Noticing my anticipation, Grams gave me a bit of a lecture: "Now as long as you stay on the ground level you can wander around in the shops, but if any workers complain about you being a pest you are going to sit your little behind on a bench where I can see you and not move an inch!"

"I swear I will behave!" I would have agreed to anything knowing that I got an hour of free rein over the mall any day, but especially if this was going to become a daily routine.

The first few trips were AMAZING. I was in heaven! I wandered from shop to shop spending the most time in the comic book store and started learning all the nooks and crannies of the Tavistock Galleria. The comic book store was small, and I tried to take my time going through the selection. I also didn't want to get kicked out for trying to read them for free, so I was always nice to the workers there. I did a lot of just wandering too though. Once I was even brave enough to go through an employee-only door, but it just led to a stinky stairwell.

We would get there as soon as it opened, nobody but us and the store employees opening up and starting their days to be seen. And even those were not as many as there should have been because only about half of the store fronts were even being used.

She only went walking on weekdays, which meant every single day that I spent with Grams started at the Tavistock Galleria. On about the 3rd week Grams started being real grumpy and made me sit on a bench even though no one had complained about me. I mean, I was starting to get bored of wandering by then. Still, I really resented having to sit and watch old ladies for an hour. I thought it was just to keep an eye on me and confirmed it when the ladies started to walk in a smaller area. Instead of walking from one end of the building to the other, they would turn around at the nail salon and come back. Losing my freedom for no apparent reason really ticked me off, so I would sit at the farthest bench I could without getting yelled at by Grams. I just couldn't understand why she had let me run free for so long only to suddenly change her mind.

Grams' grouchiness started at the house too. She would nag me about everything. It wasn't that there weren't things to nag me about, it was more that she had never told me to brush my hair, wipe my feet, put away my toys, my dishes, or any of that before. Now, she was bugging me about everything.

"I don't know why you play those games so much! You should go outside more," she'd say.

Then I would go into the backyard, and she'd start in, "Don't you trample my azaleas! You could water those plant while you are out there. And don't get muddy!"

She locked my console in the closet and when we would get back from my hour of sitting bored at the mall, I would be made to work. She had me practically clean the whole house from top to bottom. In fact, by the end of the fourth week of summer I realized Grams was the most tolerable when we were at the mall, and even there she was no longer fun at all. But, at least at Tavistock she was with her friends and not on my case. They would grumble together about how the whole town was falling apart and gossip about everyone they knew. I also noticed that they stopped talking about nice things; like how pretty their grand-babies were and those old lady topics that used to make them get all smiley.

Five weeks after it all started they began going back to the mall after lunch, so at least I got a break from cleaning for another hour a day. It was like they couldn't get enough of it! The walking path continued to get smaller though. Now they were turning by the Foot Locker. By this time, they were all pretty much just walking circles around the big blue water fountain. I gave up on my stubbornness and just sat on the wooden bench closest to the fountain and tried to read.

The fountain was a nice fixture. It felt like a safe place when everywhere else was feeling hostile to me. The sound of the old women's shoes and the water flowing from the fountain was kinda hypnotic. I started to find myself focusing on that and not my book. The whole hour would be gone in an instant and I wouldn't have read at all. This was also when I started dreaming of the fountain. I found myself wanting to go to the mall too. Instead of just something to do, it began to be all I wanted to do. I would see the fountain when I closed my eyes. I would think about it all the time. Its blue tiles, the square pedestals on the second level, and the nozzle that reminded me of Gram's bird feeder.

I would find myself wandering a huge mall-like area in my dreams; full of stores and people that I didn't recognize, and we were all looking for the fountain. I would know without a doubt that the fountain was the way out of this strange place. Each night, I would get a little closer to the sound of the water flowing and the gurgle would sound more and more like a voice. Once I started hearing the voice, I didn't know what it was saying but I need to know. That weekend I begged my mom to take me and let me read at the Tavistock Galleria, she thought I had lost my mind. I very well couldn't tell her I needed to hear what the fountain was telling me in my dreams.

"Why on earth can't you read in your room? Why do you have to do it at that crappy mall?"

I realized that 'I want to listen to the fountain' was crazy, so I didn't have anything to say back to her. Instead of shutting up like would have been smart, I let my mom know how shitty I thought she was for not taking me.

"You are just the worst Mom, ever. All you do is just leave me with Grams and sleep on the weekend. You don't do anything for me. Why don't you just drop me off at Gram's forever and forget about me. Would that make you happy?"

Needless to say, I spent that weekend grounded and really way angrier than I should have been. Monday could not come fast enough. After those weeks of being mad at Grams for her grumpiness and now here I was being mad at my Mom and I knew that Grams wanted to go to Tavistock as bad as I did so I was thrilled to be back with her for the day.

This day was a bit different though. We all met up at the fountain and I took my spot on the bench, ready to listen to the water. Grams and her friends sat on the edge of it tightening their shoe laces and catching up. Except today, nobody walked. Instead, we all just sat there. When Gale's alarm went off to signal the walk was done, we all got up and left and went our separate ways. We did the same at lunch. To be honest I don't really know whether or not the women did their walking. All I know is they were sitting in the same spots when I heard the chirper tone of Gale's alarm both times. I didn't want to leave but it was easier knowing I would be back tomorrow than it had been on Friday when I had a whole two days between me and that fountain.

That evening during diner my mom called and said she would be working a double and that I was to stay the night with Grams. Grams offered up the best idea I had heard all summer.

"How would you like to go back to the fountain after dinner, just the two of us? We can sit till closing."

I just nodded and grinned. I felt like it was Christmas.

We stopped by a convenience store and grabbed giant sodas on the way. When we got there, Grams let me sit next to her and I closed my eyes. I wanted to use all my brain power to remember what I had been enjoying so much. It took a lot of energy not to immediately be sucked into the trance, but I was able to hold on for long enough to hear a voice. It was deep and guttural but somehow soothing.

"You cannot resist, my call is true. Dig to release that which holds you."

Instead of frightening me like that voice should have, it lulled me into the trance I had been resisting.

Mom worked doubles all that week so Grams I made this our evening ritual. Her friends came and joined us too. I never asked her if she heard the voice. I heard it now on every visit and sometimes at home just before I went to sleep. I know I dreamed of the fountain, I dreamed of jumping in and the water and being taken to place deep dark place that felt like home. I arrived at the fountain in the dream mall every night by then. It always felt so nice and dark and warm and homely.

On Friday, everything changed.

When we arrived in the morning some of the workers joined us on the fountain. After lunch, more workers joined us. When we arrived after dinner there was no room to sit at the fountain, so we walked around it as Grams had in the beginning. We walked and walked and at some point, those sitting on the edge of the fountain got into the water and allowed us to sit as they walked inside.

Somewhere below a chime sounded. I was suddenly overcome by desire to destroy the fountain because it was blocking the voice. The urge to act overwhelmed me with each chime that resonated from below and vibrated the floor beneath us. I was not alone. Our crowd started trying to pry up tiles with whatever object they had on them and someone successfully knocked over the nozzle on top the fountain. Grams had pulled out a pocket knife and handed me a nail file. All I remember are flashes of us stabbing and prying as hard as humanly possible with more longing than I have ever felt before.

It is as dark, and warm, and homely as I thought it would be here in the place where the voice dwelled. The voice is no longer here, we have taken its place and would like some company, but the Tavistock Galleria has turned off the water and roped off the fountain making it harder and harder for others to hear our call.

"You cannot resist, our call is true. Dig to release that which holds you."

...but you can hear us, can't you?

# LIFE IN RETAIL

## LIFE IN RETAIL

By Charlie Davenport

I SEE ARTICLES ALL THE TIME PREDICTING THE DEATH OF traditional brick-and-mortar stores and blaming it the rise of delivery services like Amazon. There's always a twinge of sadness to those articles, like we're losing something precious as the department store and the shopping mall vanish over the horizon of yesteryear.

If you ask me, we should burn them all to the ground, salt the earth, and never look back.

I am a thoroughly average person.

I was a solid C student my entire academic career. It led me to attend a commuter college. With in-state tuition, and a meal plan furnished by Mom and Dad's fridge, I never thought money would be a major concern. That was until I found that the costs of gas and drinks with friends on Thursdays stacked up rather quickly.

The health center and the campus store were both fully staffed by the time I realized that my financial situation was

## TAVISTOCK GALLERIA

becoming dire. I came across an advertisement for a sales associate at Exxtras inside the Tavistock Galleria.

If you grew up around here between '79 and the early 2000s, you likely remember the Galleria. With half a dozen eateries, a ten screen Cineplex, and enough retail options to get a lifetime of Christmas shopping done, it was a retail juggernaut. The Lone River Mall in Haverbrook, and pretty much all of the other local competition dried up and blew away within a couple of years of Tavistock's opening.

Over the next several years, popular chains filled the mall. The food court was expanded and rechristened "Cobblestone's Cafes," and in 1993 they opened up Toppers Playground. Their mascots, a pair of clowns called Huggs and Shruggs, were the entertainment for almost every birthday party I attended between the ages of six and twelve and haunted my dreams until well past my nineteenth year.

I was there the day the Galleria opened. My mom drove around the parking lot for the better part of an hour, spotting mirage after mirage of an open parking space, before finding a real one almost half a mile from the entrance. When we finally made our way in, she *ooohed* and *aaahed* over the prices and selection offered up by the back to school sales.

It seemed that everyone within a fifty-mile radius was there that day. I got to put on a fashion show for Mom and my Aunt Silvia who took great joy in filling a dressing room with silly suits and colorful outfits and making me try on piece after piece, much to my chagrin.

"Oh! Isn't he handsome!" my aunt would exclaim.

"Such a little gentleman!" Mom would agree before making me spin around and sending me back to try on something else.

While I was being embarrassed in the Boy's section of

Montgomery Wards for hours on end, my friends were throwing dimes and quarters into the massive, multi-tiered fountain at the center of the mall. As they wolfed down slices of greasy pizza while smashing buttons at the arcade, I received pitying looks from strangers as my Mom made me try on painfully tight jeans, the kind that according to her "really made the girls take notice."

I remember these school shopping trips like they were yesterday. Mom and Aunt Silvia would pile up the clothes at the registers and the credit card machine would make that ka-chunk sound as it took a carbon impression of the numbers. But in all my life, except for trying them on in the store, I never actually wore any of those things. You would rarely see me in anything but Star Wars t-shirts and blue jeans with holes in the knees until I got to junior high school, and even then, I just traded the Star Wars t's for band shirts.

More than two decades after it opened, Tavistock's fortunes started to turn. A rumor started circulating during the 2000 Christmas season that the place was sinking, and I don't mean financially. You've all heard an old wives' tale like it before I'm sure. A college has a new library built, and before they can even complete the ribbon cutting, the building shows signs of dipping into the earth. When questioned as to how this could be happening, the embarrassed architect sheepishly admits that he hadn't taken into account the weight of the books. I've looked into it out of curiosity in the years since and while you can find a couple of messages boards with entries that amount to, "Well my cousin Dave's friend Jimmy said, that he'd heard from…"; and a section on the mall's Wikipedia confirming that it was rumored to be built on swampland, I could find no concrete evidence that verifies the sinking story. I did come across about dozen others theories that ascribe some vaguely and increasingly sinister reasons for the down turn in revenue, including some gems like these:

*It was built on a paupers' cemetery patch, a spot where those too poor in life to buy their own plot of land were laid to rest.*

*The government had found Al-Qaeda documents in Iraq that suggested Tavistock was going to be the site of their next big attack. That was a popular one during the second Gulf War.*

*A dozen or so women had disappeared from its mammoth parking lots in the space of less than three months. No bodies were ever discovered, and a police cover up was suspected.*

*The staff at the Cajun Kitchen Kiosk had a running competition to see who could get the most body hair into the customers' food without getting caught and eventually local health inspectors had caught on.*

As far as I know, none of this was true. But for whatever reason, Tavistock was all but closed by 2003. With only some of Cobblestone's vendors and few of the bigger chain stores remaining, their interior entrances now permitted admission into now dark and mostly silent halls. A couple of random merchants moved into the available space, each one selling the most haphazard collection of junk you could imagine. I remember at one point there were two different knife shops running at the same time, one in an old Build-a-Bear Workshop and another in what had been a Radio Shack.

Almost none of these little ventures lasted more than a few months, except Exxtras. It had been there for a few years by the time I pulled into the parking lot for the interview and had proved to be a moderate success among the deep discount shopping community. I'd never shopped there myself but from what Aunt Silvia had told me, it was kind of like a second-hand shop doing its best impression of a department store.

"Exxtras, we've got everything you need and a little exxtra", as their tagline said.

When I arrived for my interview, I couldn't help but glance into the mall itself. Through the glass, I could still make out the food court signage proclaiming over a dozen option of quasi-cuisine from around the world. I could see the carousel tucked into the corner of the children's play area, its fancifully colored circus animals and unicorns looking lost without anyone ready to purchase a 25-cent ride. This had been the center of the place both in both geography and spirit.

I had memories of Santa's yearly visits, complete with a live reindeer petting zoo. I also remembered kissing someone by the fountain in the center of it all. An auburn haired girl with large blue eyes. I could still feel the pressure of that girl's lips on mine, recalling it with perfect clarity but her name just kept slipping away from me. Kelli? Lauren? Or was it Heather?

I looked away, feeling inexplicably sad and guilty, as though I'd intruded on a funeral.

Exxtras seemed to be doing only moderately better than the larger body it was attached to. A small cadre of approximately fifteen retirees and single mothers diligently pushed their carts around the small maze of shelves and racks that comprised the store's various departments.

A large man standing with his feet shoulder width apart and a smile that looked like a massive series of mint Chiclets appeared in my line of sight, his booming voice inquiring cheerfully if I was,

"Ryan?"

The interview was conducted in a tiny back office by this thick slab of man, smiling the entire time, and wearing an ill-fitted brown suit and a mustard yellow dress shirt. It consisted of me answering just two questions.

Did I have any retail experience?

I'd done a weekend-only job at a hardware store during high school.

The manager, Bob as he insisted I call him, didn't seem particularly interested in any of the details about my last retail job and quickly moved on to the next question.

Would I be willing to close up at night?

I took a moment before answering.

I still wish I'd thought about it just a bit longer.

MONTHS WENT by with nothing of interest happening. I figured out what forms to fill out and got to know my new co-workers well enough to call them by their first names. I was happy to get the work. Not only did it provide me with some much needed pocket change, but there wasn't much to it beyond taking stock, taking customer complaints now and again, and tallying up the registers. That part could take some time, and it meant that I was almost always the last person to leave, but beyond that, there wasn't much to it.

Except, there was that sound.

I was sitting in the back office, rechecking the receipts from register five. Bob was pretty sure that Sherri was helping herself to a little bonus. The place was almost impossibly quiet, only the occasional rush of the water pipes broke the silence. That and the sound that was becoming impossible to ignore. I suspect that it had been there for quite some time in the background before it forced itself to some forward region of my brain. I set my pen aside and craned my neck like Elmer Fudd listening for the wascally wabbit.

*Scritch. Scratch.*

"What is that?" I said aloud to the mismatched collection of naked and unused mannequins positioned around me.

It wasn't steady or even vaguely constant, which would have suggested some poorly maintained mechanism trudging through its own functions. No, it was several beats in a steady, if off-beat rhythm punctuated by long silences.

"Rats." I thought with a shudder of revulsion.

My mother was terrified of the things, constantly sick with the notion that the furry little bastards had somehow made their way into our home. I honestly think I saw the exterminator in my kitchen more than any plumber or electrician. Fleshy tails, disease ridden bodies, and teeth that if left unchecked by constant gnawing will plunge upwards into their own brains… I could not think of the foul little things as just living creatures like any other.

*Scritch. Scratch.*

Sherri's receipts and take for the day matched, near as I could tell. If she was stealing from the

store, she was good at it. I swung the door of the ancient safe open and tossed the deposit bag inside before slamming it shut again. The sound abruptly ceased as if whatever made it had been startled by the clang of the metal.

"Rats." I said again to myself with finality, as though I had to confirm it.

Suddenly very eager to leave the store, I got my coat from

my locker in the breakroom and headed to the front. Through the large window I could see the yellow-white sodium lights illuminating the parking lot, my car the only one still occupying a spot.

*Scritch.*

*Scritch. Scratch.*

*Scritch. Scratch. Scritch. Scratch.*

*Scritch. Scratch. Scritch. Scratch. Scritch. Scratch.*

They say that for every rat or mouse you see or hear there are easily a dozen more. The thought that I was in the center of some gigantic nest of the things came very close to making me bolt straight out into the night, job or no. While I wrestled with my natural fear and disgust of the hairy invaders, the sound dropped away and there was a profound silence. I stood absolutely still, fearing that any movement would set them off again.

*Scritch.*

I flew to the door, hitting the release bar with my whole body, crashing against it and the glass. It was only once I was outside that any degree of rational thought came back to me and I had enough sense to steady my hand long enough to lock the place up.

I sat in front of the TV and sipped bourbon most of the night. Eventually the drone of the screen and the slow trickle of alcohol lulled my brain enough that I could consider going to bed. I was feeling more than a little embarrassed at how much I had freaked out as I settled in for the evening and before I knew it my alarm was going off. I decided to stop by the store and inform Bob of the pest problem before I headed off to my first class.

"Boss Man, there's coming in early and then there's just being an oddball." Sherri, of register five fame, stared in mild amazement at me as I walked into the store with the sunshine on my shoulders. The mother of two chortled as she straightened the shock of Manic Panic purple hair out of her eyes. She leaned in and stage whispered to the nicotine-stained woman waiting for her change, "Ma'am don't be alarmed but that young man is the assistant manager." The old lady cracked a smile in my direction.

"Hey Sherri." I said. The rough crack in my voice made me realize she was the first person I'd actually spoken to that day. "Is Bob in?"

"Yeah, just like most days." Sherri finished ringing up the old lady and planting her hands on either side of her station, leaned forward to appraise me. "Anyone tell you that you look like absolute shit?"

"Yeah, my Mom's good for that kind of thing. He in the back?"

"Nope." Sherri pointed to the far western corner of the store. Standing among that retail detritus was Bob, easily spotted at his six-foot six height and clad in his mustard shirt, just as he had been the day he hired me.

"Thanks."

I made my way through the racks of half-off winter gear, reflecting not for the first time that Bob had far too much stuff jammed into far too little space. This place had to violate a number of fire codes. As I continued weaving, I heard it again.

*Scritch.*

A single noise that could have easily come from me rubbing past one of the racks and dragging a resistant hanger across its railing.

"Bob." I called out.

He turned, an odd look stretched across his ham-colored

features. In those brief periods we met when his work day was ending and mine was just beginning, I'd never really seen much in the way of emotion pass over Bob's face. This expression of what I wanted to call confusion sat uncomfortably on his features, like he'd been pumped full of Novocain and couldn't really feel what his face was doing. For a moment I became convinced that Bob just hadn't recognized me.

"It's me, Ryan." and then I stupidly gestured towards my own chest as though further clarification was needed.

*Scritch. Scratch.*

"Yes?" He said with a quizzical tilt of his head, indicating that he still wasn't clear on how my identity might be relevant to the rest of his day. "How can I help you?"

"Oh. OK. Right." I said sagely. "So I was closing up last night and I heard a noise."

Bob raised his eyebrows in a rough and badly rendered approximation of human interest. "Kind of sounded like we might have a..."

"Ryan, you've been a great help to me and the boys upstairs," he gestured with his index finger towards the ceiling which as far as I knew didn't have anything above it besides an unused second floor, "have really taken notice as well." He looked back at me clearly anticipating some form of response.

Not knowing what else to do I just said, "Um, thank you Bob. I, I appreciate that."

I watched his mouth open up into his trademark smile, which possessed all the warmth of a corpse with dentures. He turned to walk away, clearly feeling our conversation was over.

"I think we might have rats, Bob." I said.

Bob stopped walking instantly and stood with his back

to me for a moment. Then he suddenly spun on his heel, and I was once again faced with that perfect and unsettling smile.

"What are you suggesting Ryan?"

"Well, I don't know the procedure in situations like this. Is there someone the company uses for this kind of thing? If you'd like me to deal with getting in touch with them I can do that."

In the time it had taken me to speak, Bob had closed the gap between us and now stood very much within my personal space.

"No you misunderstand me. I was not asking what you were suggesting we do. I'm asking if you," he thumped me with a thick sausage of an index finger in my clavicle hard enough to produce a hollow thump, "are suggesting that there is some kind of problem in my store, something amiss, that I am unaware of."

His surprisingly solid digit planted itself on the edge of soft tissue and bone once again, a mixture of hot rage and shame burned at the tips of my ears.

"Are you suggesting that I am not doing my job?" Thump went his finger a third time into the same spot. "Are you in fact suggesting that you might be better for this position than me?" He left his index finger there against my chest, exerting just the slightest hint of forward pressure.

Thinking back on it, I don't believe he ever stopped smiling during that entire exchange. "No, sir. That's not what I am saying at all."

*Scritch. Scratch.*

My head snapped in the direction of that noise and I knew I'd made a terrible and fatal mistake. I'd taken my eyes off of Bob and he certainly was going to take that opportunity to open that stupid smile just as wide as it would go and make a quick meal of me.

I pulled my gaze back to my manager and I found that, while all of his teeth were still on display there was no indication he planned to go cannibal.

"Good, Ryan. As I was saying, I think you have a real future here with us."

Then he just turned on his heel and strode off for some other part of the store. Occasionally he would nod or raise his hand in greeting at no one in particular. I watched him until he was out of sight and then stood there for a while in confusion, wondering just what the hell had transpired. But except for Bob being a supremely odd bird, and maybe a bit overstressed by his position, I could come up with nothing.

I said nothing to Sherri as I left the store and went to school.

The rest of the day was uneventful. I went to my econ class then drove home to grab a bite to eat and change before heading back into work. Mom and Dad were just getting home from their respective jobs and had enough time to ask in passing how my day had gone. I gave the same routinely generic answers I always did, choosing to say nothing of rats or of Bob and his finger. My Mom did ask how I'd slept, saying she thought she'd heard me through the wall sounding as though I'd tossed and turned the entire night. I told her I was fine and kissed her on the cheek.

I got to work a little early and set about the exciting routine of a retail assistant manager. There were the standard customer complaints and returns, explaining to a couple of people why they couldn't use coupons from other stores. The normal stuff. I was in the back doing paper work, leaving my door open for some much needed ventilation. I saw Sherri drift by, already in her street clothes, heading to the clock to punch out.

"Sherri?" I called out and was rewarded with her sticking her head back through the door, warm smile on her face.

"Yesss Boss Man?"

"Please stop calling me that."

"Yes Boss Man." She deadpanned and then let her face slowly slide back into a grin "We like ourselves, don't we Sherri?" I couldn't help but smile back.

It was only in her smile, in the way the flesh crinkled around her eyes when she did it, that would clue anyone in that she was five years older than me. Two kids on this salary couldn't be easy and still you never doubted that her smile was a genuine expression of joy. I don't think I realized it then but I'm pretty sure I had a mild crush on her. Everybody was fond of Sherri, customers and staff alike. In fact, the only person I could think of that didn't seem to take to her was Bob.

"Indeed we do."

I was quiet for a moment, uncertain of how to phrase it.

"Were you going to ask me something or did you just want a change of scenery?" "How was Bob today?"

The smile snapped off of her face in an instant.

"Fine I guess; why do you ask?"

"Well, did he act strange? Strange for Bob I mean." "Good catch."

"Thanks."

"Not really. After you talked to him," She looked back behind her before continuing, "I didn't really see him again." She suddenly looked uncomfortable.

"Did he seem agitated?"

"Hey, I gotta go pick up the kids from my Mom's." She

looked apologetic but was clearly done with this conversation. "She's great for making sure they get decent meal but helping with homework is not her thing."

"No, sure, I understand," and then I reflexively threw in, "Sorry."

"No, no thing." She hurried back out into the hall and I heard the solid punch of the clock indicating that her day at Exxtras was done.

She passed by my door again, the clomp of her boots echoing on the floor as she kept her eyes forward.

"Hey Ryan?"

I looked up from my paperwork and saw her standing in my door again, looking very uncertain. "Yeah, what's up?"

"Listen I like you, so I'm going to tell you something I probably shouldn't."

"OK." I said. She had my full attention.

"I wouldn't ask too many question about Bob. He's never said anything directly to me but it all gets back to him."

"What do you mean?"

"I made a comment about needing some extra cash for daycare and Carl heard it as 'Exxtra's Cash.'" She grimaced.

Carl was a sweet kid but he was the sort that truly believed some Nigerian prince was going to send him money and a quick blast of flatulence was always going to be the funniest thing in the world to him.

"Oh."

"Yeah, next thing I know someone jokes about me getting a five-finger discount started and eventually it got back to Bob. All I'm saying is this place has ears and Bob is…" She rubbed a spot just above her breast. I wondered in Bob had a similar conversation with her as he did with me.

"Did he…?"

"I need this job. You'd probably be fine without it but if you're planning to stick around, I wouldn't poke the bear."

She smiled again and said her goodbyes, even throwing in that she thought I was a great kid. I felt a surprising twinge of disappointment at that comment and considered reminding her there was only five years between us, but she was already down the hall.

*All I'm saying is this place has ears.*

Sherri was gone by the time I made it to the front. She was the last one out and I had to lock the door behind her. I looked out over the lot and as always was stunned at how dark it had gotten. Time in the back office seemed to move differently than out front. What felt like just a few minutes in there could easily having you greeting full nightfall when you were expecting dusk at most. I put the key back in my pocket and headed for the office. I wanted to be out of here before there was any chance I'd hear…

*Scritch. Scratch.*

I looked around, but I was in one of the few open display areas in the store, so there was nowhere for a rodent to hide. Where had the sound come from?

An overhead fixture shone down a beam of light filled with dust motes. In the center of the beam was a single mannequin. It wore a puffy quilted jacket zipped up to the top paired with a set of khaki cargo shorts, and his blocky feet had been shoved into a pair of laceless canvas shoes. On its face was a pair of knockoff Ray-Bans, shielding its eyes from the pale fluorescence of the store. All that was missing was a sign at the bottom that identified it as a museum-quality representation of the "North American Bro." The plastic man held its petrified hands splayed slightly out at its sides as if acknowledging the ridiculousness of its attire, if not its existence. I looked up at that ageless face, bathed in light as it was.

*Scritch.*

Was the rat hiding in the mannequin?

I drew closer and closer until I was standing almost nose to nose with the plastic thing. I waited to hear the sound and hoped that I wouldn't. Still reeling from the encounter with Bob, I wondered if I should just leave it alone. After all, the store was his responsibility, not mine. I'd reported it and he'd responded the way he had. In the end, I was just a part-time paperwork clerk, and no matter how good a job the 'boys upstairs' thought I was doing, I had no plans to go anywhere with this company.

The mannequin stared impassively as I waited, motionless, for the creature to reveal itself. The sound had definitely come from the dummy and despite my revulsion or having any idea how I was going to do it, I was determined to catch or kill the vermin, just to prove to Bob that I had been right and that he had been a jerk to dismiss me so rudely.

*Scritch.*

It was in the head.

I went around the mannequin looking for the hole that let the creature in and out. If I could trap the pest inside, I could open it in the morning and show that we had rats nesting in the store. I came back around to face it.

*Scritch.*

I pulled off its glasses and looked into its painted-on eyes. Except these weren't painted on. There was something different here. Had the rats chewed a hole in the—-

Suddenly, between its eternally open lids, eyes rolled in their sockets to focus on me.

I took a reflexive step back, and as much as I tried not to

look at the plastic man's eyes, I couldn't help but be fascinated by them. They rubbed against the confines of that artificial skull, scraping inside it with a sick, flicking desperation. That two-tone chorus accompanying each movement.

*Scritch. Scratch.*

It was only a matter of seconds before some primitive, animal part of me pushed me away and I ran. I blundered down an aisle that I'd walked a dozen or more times, one I knew that lead to the front door. Except it didn't.

Directly in front of me there was a column of black winter coats, the kind intended for wear in early January on the tundra. To my left there was a bank of threadbare brown suits, exuding a scent like a funeral parlor, antiseptic chemicals and rot. I turned in circles trying to find a way out, or at least the way I'd come from. In the distance for miles on either side were just sets of repeating pants, jackets, and those damn wool overcoats. I was boxed in, lost in a canyon of cast off jackets and irregular pants. Despite knowing that this was impossible, I felt a spike of pure panic hit me between my shoulders.

Eventually I came upon a narrow gap between two shelves, and squeezing through it I found a legless female mannequin arching its back in a permanent rictus while holding a golf club aloft behind its head. Somehow I'd found my way into sporting goods. I felt relief for a minute but then I heard the grinding of two painted orbs forcing themselves to the edge of its vision. In my panic I smacked into displays of sporting equipment, pin balling down row after row until eventually my foot caught on something I had dislodged from the shelves. I was sent sprawling. I came to a stop at the feet of a couple playing tennis. Their rackets raised as if each meant to deliver a blow to the neck of the other. A light sprinkling of dust capered down onto my prone form from their ocular sockets.

*Scritch. Scratch.* The sound ringing out above me in perfect stereo.

A bright red kickball fell from the hands of something that was intended to look like a small boy and rolled in front of my path. Its fingers remained outstretched as if to snatch at whomever might pass by.

*Scritch.*

A pair of businessmen stopped eternally midstride and mid-conversation took note as I bolted past.

*Scratch.*

An entire nuclear family, the kind that had only existed on 1950s sitcoms, sat around a plaid

blanket with an open picnic basket between them. The plaster bounty laid out before them, uneaten.

*Scritch. Scratch.*

I registered a brownish blur in my path. I struck it full on and crashed backwards again onto the tiles. An unmistakably male figure in a baggy brown suit towered over me, baring its teeth at me. I heard that now familiar screeching, like fingernails deliberately drawn over a chalkboard. It forced its unliving eyes down to take me in and I saw a spot of brownish red smeared across its mustard yellow dress shirt.

Bob.

*Bob was never a real boy.* The thought popped into my head and I nearly laughed out loud.

All it would take was one more good shove of the impossible to process, and I would be a gibbering mess the rest of my life. If I stayed there even one second more, I knew the Bob Thing was going to speak. Some recognizable word, or even worse my name, would escape from somewhere inside him and there would be no going back.

I scrambled up and found myself in front of a pair of doors. Somehow in my panic I had found the way out! The doors did not resist in the slightest as I pushed them open, but instead of depositing me out into the open air, I spilled out near the Epoch Cineplex, posters for *Rise of the Machines* and *The Last Samurai* were still up on the walls. They looked as though they'd just been placed there, save for a layer of dust that covered them. I did not dwell on it for long because as soon as I emerged from the store, the sense of being pursued ceased, but I did not stop moving, nor did I look back.

I navigated using the "You Are Here" directory maps that had been placed at various points in the mall. According to them there was an exit out to the east lot over by Toppers. I joked in my own head that at this point I was willing to risk the chance of seeing Huggs and Shruggs again if it meant that I might be able to get out of there. I made my way past a dozen dark hallways and display windows, some with their own mannequins still within them, most newer than those in Exxtras. Completely smooth with only the slightest, almost impressionistic hint of facial features.

I APPROACHED the center of the mall. The fountain, still an extraordinarily large, multi-tiered thing, had long since been drained of its water and was instead filled with random bits of cardboard, twine, and plastic wrapping. In the middle of this very odd day, I stopped. With the exterior door only a dozen yards away, I was suddenly overcome with a penetrating sense of sadness. This place deserved better didn't it? People had done more than just buy things here; they'd made memories here. It wasn't fair. This place was being tossed aside. No longer allowed to be the grand thing that it had earned the right to be. Something was calling to me beneath the tiles and refuse, something that needed my attention, my notice. This place wasn't just cold commerce was it? The memory of that kiss, not my first kiss, but a sweet, fleeting moment between two awkward teenagers, proved that. This place had a heartbeat, and I fancied that I could even feel it under my feet. Maybe I could do something, even if it was only a small thing. It would just take a little while to dig some of that garbage out of the fountain. Yeah, just get all of that out of there and then I could be on my way knowing I had properly paid my debt to this wonderful place.

*Scritch.*

I whirled around and found that I was no longer alone. Some of the featureless things were pressed up against the glass of empty store windows, their perfectly smooth hands pressed against the barrier in an act of supplication. Others were at a distance down side corridors, making the pilgrimage from the storage rooms, dumpsters, and the back passageways of the mall. Still more were arched around in a semi-circle around the fountain itself. They did not move in any perceivable way, but with every passing second there were more of them. Two were there had been one, three where there had been two. Something was calling to these breathless mockeries, something that needed their notice. Their worship. Something that lived and breathed in that fountain. No other sound accompanied this unseen gathering, no clack of their toeless bare feet against the concrete. No sound but the chorused scrape of their eyes, those never living eyes rasping against their limits, as they closed in upon me.

I don't fully recall everything that followed. I have some memory of smashing glass and the impact of rigid digits trying to force themselves around my limbs and clothing. I awoke in my bed with the light of afternoon streaming in through the window. I was wearing my clothes from the night before and I had deep scratches on my forearms and legs.

I don't suppose that any of you will be surprised to learn that I never went back there. Not for work or even general curiosity. I didn't give two weeks' notice and I think I still have the key to the store's front door somewhere among the things I've collected in my life. Thinking about it now I should probably try and find it, just so I can drive to the nearest big body of water and toss the damn thing into it. I buckled down in my studies, brought my GPA up and shortly thereafter transferred out of state. My Mom and Dad, while worried about me moving so far away, were pleased with this new drive I'd found.

"I know what did it." My Dad had said with a smile over a steak dinner the night before I left for UCLA. "Didn't want to spend the rest of your life at the mall, did you Ryan?"

It's been a lot of years since then. I graduated, got a job, got married, and had kids. I did all the things that constitute a life, and I can say with all honesty that it's been a good one. I have never encountered anything like that ever again, but sometimes…

Going shopping, I mean physically going to a store, is quickly going the way of the automat and dial up internet, but now and again, something will come up that requires me to go to a big box store or God forbid, a mall. It's usually an anniversary that crept up on me, or it's my turn to go pick up the congratulatory gift for someone at the office. They're there of course. I don't make eye contact with them. I can't have word getting back to Tavistock.

I can hear them you see. I can hear them observing me as I try to blend in with the other shoppers. Yes, I can hear them and I think they know it.

*Scritch.*

CLOSING DAY

CLOSING DAY

By William Stuart

**Prologue: 1994**

"Going to lunch, guys, see you in 30!"

"See you, Heather."

My new shoes squeaked on the newly polished tile as I approached the cluster of shoppers lined up for the elevator.

"One flight. How lazy can you be?" I thought as I took the stairs on the way down to the food court.

It was an unusually busy Saturday in the Tavistock Galleria, but nobody seemed to mind. This was business at its finest: happy shoppers with money to spend getting up early, driving, parking, and waiting in lines to meet with clerks and salespeople happy to take it off them. Kids crowded the arcade, standing in lines to play the newest games while their parents wandered the halls lost in nearly a square mile of climate-controlled commerce.

"Morning, Heather!"

"Hey, Kenney," I said to the guy out in front of Sam Goody. *Don't be weird. Don't be weird. Don't be weird...* I commanded myself as I stopped to talk to the tall, smiling guy; his longish, *perfect* hair hanging in his eyes, "how's it going?"

Kenney shrugged and looked around, keeping his hands tucked in his company-issued black apron. "Kind of busy today. You?"

"Yeah."

"Excuse me," said a man as he passed through the crowd. He bumped my shoulder and shoved me right into my crush! Kenney's hands came out of the apron and he caught me as I stumbled.

"You okay?" Kenney smiled, showing genuine concern as I caught my balance. He then called out, "Hey! Watch it, mister!"

Mortified, I felt my face go flush. I stammered for a second before finding my words. "Well, um, got to, you know, get in the line before I miss lunch," I shrugged and tried to smile, "Um, see you later?"

"Um, sure," Kenney said, sensing something was wrong, "I mean, like, don't worry about that guy. He's just a dick. I mean, okay?"

"Of course. Screw that guy. I mean, I just have to go. You know. My break."

Kenney smiled warmly and shrugged, "I can't leave because we're short this week but maybe next time we can go to lunch together?"

I nearly stumbled into a passing shopper as I nodded in shock. This was what I had been waiting for since the first time I'd seen Kenney. He'd been so cool and confident and with the hair and the bit of a slouch, just that proper amount of good and bad boy. I'm not going to lie, I'd been completely smitten since the first time I'd seen him. And I did my best each day to find a reason to pass by the record store, hoping that he'd be there; maybe just to see him through the window as he talked to customers or stocked CDs.

I managed to croak a not-so-casual, "Sure," before continuing my way to lunch. I daydreamed as I walked, barely noticing the ever-increasing number of shoppers everywhere. The bustle of the mall was beginning to seem more like a crowded subway than a shopping center.

When I arrived at the food court, my first thought was to Chick-Fil-A, where I knew the manager and could usually get a hookup on some fries. But the lines were all impossibly long. I glanced down the hall at the McDonald's. They were even busier.

*Where did all these people come from?* Was there some kind of event today that I wasn't aware of? I cast about desperately looking for any restaurant I could hope to get a meal from before my break was over. Sbarro? Full. Taco Bell? Packed. Even the weird little Greek place down the way was staring down a line of customers twenty deep.

*What the hell?*

I'd never seen the mall this busy before. And what was more, the shoppers seemed... *off* somehow. Among the more casual Saturday shoppers were people dressed very nicely-men in suits and women in dresses, as if they just got out of church. Others wandered around staring at some kind of glowing light-up thing in their hands. I felt my head to make sure I didn't have a fever. Something was definitely not right all of a sudden.

*Is that guy smoking?*

Sure enough, there stood a man who looked to be in his late twenties. He was dressed in a dark colored suit and tie.

He leaned against a pillar and took heavy drags off a cigarette, in full disregard for the NO SMOKING sign on the wall just six inches above his head. He caught me staring and glanced over, tipping his hat politely as he smiled. I tried to smile back and then backed up and turned to go the other way.

I weaved in and out between shoppers who all seemed unperturbed by the crowded situation. I eventually found a space where I could see across the entire court. Countless shoppers milled about, some waiting in line for food, while others strolled casually in every direction. Finally, I just gave up. Whatever was going on, it didn't look like I was going to be able to grab a bite before going back to work. I slouched, defeated, and moved into the thrall back in the direction of the stairs.

I'd only gone a few paces when something caught my eye. There, in the corner near the Greek place, was a shop with no line! I moved to the side to let an old couple pass and looked again. The sign was orange with a little devil cherub holding a pitchfork.

"Orange Julius," I said aloud. This was weird. I remembered this place from when I was a kid, but hadn't they had all gone out of business? There was no line, though, so I decided to give it a try.

"Good afternoon, ma'am," said the girl behind the counter.

"Hi. Um, You just open?"

The girl looked at me strangely and said, "No ma'am, nine o' clock, like always."

"I meant your shop. Haven't seen it before."

The girl wore a blue and orange uniform with the devil logo and a blue and orange visor with the same. I glanced from the devil on the shirt to the one on the hat to the one on the sign above the girl's head. There was something unnerving about it, but I didn't know what. "Can I get you something?"

"Um, I guess I'll try the Orange Julius."

"Yes ma'am, small or large?"

"Do you have a medium?"

The girl shot me a glance and then said, "We only have two sizes. Small or large."

"I'll take a large, please."

The girl nodded, then called to a peer, "One large!" before punching the keys on the register. "That will be forty-one cents, please."

"Uh, okay. Running a special?" I said as I dug through my purse for change.

"Special what?"

"Never mind." I stared at my hands for a moment before an older teenager in the same shirt and visor combo placed my cup on the counter.

"One large," he said before turning back to his machine.

"Thank you, ma'am, please have a nice day."

I just nodded and took my cup and began walking back to the store. The crowd seemed to be thinning a bit and by the time I made it back to the stairs, the mall was only about half as busy as it had been just a few minutes before. The second floor was nearly deserted when I made it to the landing. I looked out over the balcony, a sudden uneasy feeling having come over me. The first floor was still packed, and I took a sudden, unexplainable solace in that.

I sipped on the creamy orange drink as I walked, keeping my eyes on the throngs of shoppers below moving to and fro to wherever their Saturday shopping would take them. When I arrived at my shop, I turned into it without looking and walked face-first into the security gate, spilling my drink all over myself.

*What the hell?*

I stepped backward and looked at the empty store front, then up and down the corridor. I'd gotten off the elevator at the wrong floor before and walked this far down before realizing it, but I think I would have noticed having gone up a whole extra flight of stairs. I looked up at the sign, an old and dusty bit of broken neon that had just, half-an-hour before, been lit, hanging over a store full of people and lights and merchandise. Now the cavern was dark and empty save for some long-forgotten slat-wall pegs and broken shelving. In the window to the left of the gate was posted a sign.

"Please excuse our mess while we remodel to better serve you.
Another of your favorite stores coming Summer, 2004.

*2004? Is this some kind of joke?*

I stumbled backward, crushed cup still in my hand and sticky orange drink dripping from my shirt and khaki pants. I stared at the sign, then up and down the corridor. Everything was wrong. The carpet was different. No, that wasn't right. *There had been no carpet!* I didn't recognize any of the stores. My heart raced, and I took deep breaths to stave off panic.

I'd gone to the wrong floor. That was it. I'd blanked out for a second and with all the people and the weirdness, I'd simply gone up an extra floor on autopilot and ended up in front of a store with a misprinted sign. I calmed myself down and made my way back toward the stairs, tossing the sticky cup in the trash bin as I passed.

Down one floor, I knew I hadn't been mistaken. This was the food court level. Shoppers still crammed in the filtered sunlight coming through the glass windows fifty feet above. I turned from the food court and ran back toward the stairs. I had missed something.

Kenney! I should have passed the record store on my way back here, but I hadn't seen it. I jogged through shoppers, searching for the sign. Panic had set in now and tears were flowing freely as I searched for the orange neon of the Sam Goody store front. I went to where it should have been but instead it was a maternity store. A kind-looking woman stood near the front setting up sale tags and smiled at me as I passed.

I stopped. I would ask that woman what was going on and see if I could use their phone to call my dad to come pick me up. I turned on my heels and jogged back to the maternity store and then fell to my knees when instead of a well-lit store, it too was darkened with a "Pardon our Dust" sign and a lowered security gate blocking entrance to the empty cavern beyond.

I fell to my knees and screamed until my lungs gave out. Occasionally, shoppers passed and glanced down at me before moving on to another store. Others stepped over me like I wasn't even there at all.

"Sir? Sir, can you hear me?"

I opened my eyes to an impossibly bright light. There were people all around me, but I couldn't make any of them out. They were just silhouettes against a painfully white background. My head. Oh god, did my head hurt. I tried to cooperate, to answer, to do anything, but instead I just lay back and put my arm across my eyes to shield them from the light.

"Talk to me, sir, can you understand me?"

I heard snapping fingers and the quiet hush of concerned onlookers. Whoever this was that was talking to me needed me to respond. Fine. I raised my other hand and gave him a thumbs-up before letting it rest again.

"Good, good. We're gonna get you to a hospital, okay? Just lie here and take it easy. The ambulance will be here in a bit."

Another raised thumb. More painful throbbing in my head. My lower lip was swollen and sore and I could feel the cut and taste a little blood.

What happened?

It was just another job. Nothing special about it. Just survey the property, take note of on-premise assets, and sign some documents. In and out and on the plane. Hell, if I could finagle my time well enough and get the client's representatives to meet early, I could catch the early flight and be home early enough to beat traffic. All in a day's work.

Except it wasn't just another job and there was something special about it. There was something missing. I had taken the hotel shuttle to the property and…

I can see my shoes stepping out of the van and onto the pavement and then…

I am on my back with unbearable light in my eyes despite their being covered by my arm. Someone is talking to me; says there's an ambulance on the way. My head is pounding. Worse than the worst headache I've ever had. And throbbing too. Fresh shocks of pain thrumming with the rhythm of my pulse.

What is going on? What happened? Did I have a stroke?

I think of the man with the crooked face. The crooked faced man stares back at me as the doctor lubes up his gloved finger for "that" test. That most uncomfortable of checkups.

That one you never think you'll ever be old enough to get until one day you are and for a second, an impossibly long second there's a finger in your ass and you're staring at this man whose face is normal on one half, but the other half is fallen and distorted like the old comic book villain whose name escapes me now.

"Know the signs of stroke," it says; the little trifold flyer in the acrylic box next to other informative trifold flyers warning of other horrible diseases and conditions.

But now I'm on my back, unable to stand the light. I don't know where I am, or why, or even who. Did I have a stroke? Is this how it ends?

The light began to fade a bit and with it, the pain. Although it was still excruciating, it was made bearable by the passing seconds. I could still hear the people around me speaking in worried whispers and I became aware that I was laying on broken rocks or gravel. Had I simply fallen and bumped my head? I removed my arm from across my eyes and tried to see what was around me. A gaggle of worried shoppers stood in a circle a distance away, clutching their packages and murmuring to one another.

"What happened?" Asked a heavy-set woman with thick makeup.

"Dunno," said a woman next to her, "He was just there."

"Where did all the glass come from?" Asked someone else.

"Somebody must have hit him with something," said yet another person, "Did anybody check his wallet?"

As they spoke, I could see their faces more clearly. There were men and women, girls and boys, and somewhere, the sound of rushing water echoed as if running in a large room. These details and others began to coalesce into an answer to at least one of my questions. Where was I? I scanned the crowd for a familiar face, hoping to find a friend or associate who could help. What was going on?

Then, impossibly loud against the din of the shoppers and the fountain, the snap-click and flick of a Zippo lighter.

No.

It hadn't been a stroke at all. All at once, I remembered. And with every little bit of strength I had left, I rolled to my feet and ran.

∼

"Mister Erickson?" said the man extending his hand as I climbed out of the shuttle, "Welcome to Tavistock. I'm James Wilcox, the property manager. How was your flight?"

I adjusted my Ray Bans and then took his hand to shake. "Not bad, not bad. I do have to say, it's quite weird coming here today."

Wilcox grimaced and looked over his shoulder as we walked into the building. "Yes, it is quite the shame, isn't it? The death of retail. But who can compete?" He then turned his head to me and said, "Bet you're keeping quite busy these days, aren't you?"

"You know, when I started, it was rare occasion that an entire mall would go full under. But I've been doing this for quite a while. And unfortunately, we're getting busier every year."

"Damn kids with their phones and their digital downloads. We used to chase them off, discourage them. Hell, we'd even hand pick music we thought was, uncool, just to keep the kids out." He shrugged and then shook his head sadly. "Damn it if it didn't work."

Our footsteps echoed in the largely empty caverns of the

mall as we made our way to Wilcox's office. There we would meet the other trustees and attorneys and sign the paperwork that would officially end more than forty years of business for the fading behemoth.

It was always a strange place, a dying mall. There are always two or three of the big anchor stores left at the far ends of long hallways and balconies lined with dark store fronts and security gates. As we walked, I noticed that the gates were down in many central areas of the mall as well, meaning that entire wings were closed off and secured. The high ceilings with their giant skylights allowed most of the indoor center to be lit naturally, with the lights from the stores filling in the gaps and enhancing the shopping experience. But with all the darkened store fronts, the mall was an eerie dark place interspersed with light here and there, like the caves you see in nature shows. Add to that the canned retail jazz that was still being pumped into the deserted areas where it echoed and distorted and you had a pretty creepy place.

As we walked, the mall became brighter and when we turned into the food court, there was a surprisingly large crowd gathered, carrying shopping bags and lining up for lunch. Children rode on the large imported carousel and the few remaining restaurants had decent lines in front.

"Final clearance on most things," Wilcox muttered, "Officially, we're here 'till the end of the year, but everyone's paid up so there's nothing stopping them from pulling out early if they can clear their inventories. Save on payroll hours. Here we are."

We turned into a hallway that opened into an office suite with several cubicles and conference rooms. Wilcox went to one of these and opened the door. "Good morning everyone, this is Mr. Erickson and he'll be facilitating the business today. Should be pretty quick and painless, I think."

I walked around shaking hands as Wilcox took a seat and began shuffling a pile of papers. There were twelve of them; smartly-dressed, middle-aged men and women in expensive suits and skirts. They each took my hand in turn and we all did the fake smile/nod thing you do when you're a professional, but you don't really like or trust one another. They took their seats and I removed a stack of files from my bag and had them passed around.

"Good morning," I began, "I know that this is a day you all hoped would never come. I'm Ken Erickson and I am the buyer's representative. I would like for each of you to review the documents and ensure that everything is in order."

I dug into the front pocket of my shoulder bag and pulled out a flash drive. I placed it into the projector on the desk and started the slide show. The first slide was an aerial view of the mall complex as it stands today, all concrete and glass. I went to the next slide- a digital artist's rendering of mixed-use development that would replace Tavistock after the close.

High-end apartments sat above retail and restaurants in a simulated town square. Children played in secure green spaces while a band played—not too loudly mind you—to their gleeful parents. Parking garages flanked the superstructure, but instead of the normal white and grey concrete, these were painted with trees and animals to give it a more natural look in these days of environmental concern.

"This, ladies and gentlemen, is what we plan to do with the property. As you know, we are not just in the business of tearing things down. There is a rich and storied history here. So many great memories. So many firsts. We want to make sure that the spirit, that the memory of Tavistock is still alive and well, and not paved over.

"I'm sure you can imagine, as I can, how many thousands of people have passed through these doors in the past forty years. How many first dates, how many prom dresses, how many tuxedos. We take these sorts of things seriously, folks. We have nothing but respect for the legacy of this mall. Nations have risen and fallen while the fountains in the Tavistock Galleria has flowed. And I don't think any of you know this, but this place has a special place in my heart. It's true. My very first job was here at the Tavistock when I was sixteen years old."

The suits looked up from their contracts to stare at me. Until now, I was just another corporate shark, sent to take ownership of their beloved mall. Now, their expressions changed. They softened.

"Where did you work?" one asked.

"The Sam Goody record store near the food court."

"I thought Sam Goody was on three," said another.

"They moved to three in those last couple of years before they closed down for good," said a third, "But before that they were on the mezzanine."

The atmosphere became more personable and friendly and within a few minutes, I had all my documents signed and the meeting was adjourned. We milled about for a few minutes making small talk and I checked my phone to see if I couldn't get an earlier flight, but no such luck. Wilcox came and shook my hand, visibly relieved to have the whole ordeal behind him.

"Well, Mr. Erickson, as much as it pains me to say, it's been nice doing business with you. You have a nice way about you. Do you tell the same story in every city?"

"Excuse me?" I asked, confused, "What story?"

"About working in the mall as a teenager. It was a nice touch."

"Well, I did. When I was sixteen I worked in the record store. It was right over there," I pointed across the food court toward one of the darkened corridors, "For almost a year."

Wilcox furrowed his brow and scratched his head. "Huh, well I'll be damned. I can see what you mean about it being weird coming here today. Nobody from your office mentioned that."

"Well, it was a long time ago," I said, "But when this project came up, I had to be sure it was I who made the trip. Some of my best days were spent right over there sorting CD's. I don't think there's a cooler job for a teenager to have than a record store. Too bad they're mostly all gone too." I shrugged, "Just wanted to say goodbye to the old girl."

"Well, I'm glad you got the chance," he said. "Anyway, you probably have a plane to catch. Thank you again for making the process so simple. It helped take away some of the pain."

"Sure thing. Look, my flight's not for several hours. Mind if I wander around for a while? I've got a nostalgia itch that wants to be scratched. "

"Knock yourself out," he shrugged, "It's technically yours anyway. Watch out when you go through doors. You may get locked on the other side and would have to find an exit and walk all the way around to get back in."

We shook hands and I thanked him for his hospitality. He gave me a strange look as if trying to place me from somewhere, then shook his head and made off back toward the hall that led to the offices. I walked to one of the few remaining restaurants and waited in a slow-moving line for an iced tea. Then, drink in hand, I wandered off toward where my old store had been nearly twenty-five years before.

It's a strange thing visiting old haunts. For one, everything is much smaller than you remember. When I was a kid, my folks would bring me to the mall and it seemed like the hallways went on forever. Everything was so modern and clean, brightly-lit, and massive. It was still massive, but it was much less so to this cynical forty-something than it had been to the eight-year-old who would come with his mom; a mom that was so impressed with the mall's grandeur that she never let me leave her sight for fear that we'd get separated and she'd never see me again.

When I'd worked here, the place gave up many of its secrets, such as the hallways and freight elevators that ran behind the stores. You really got to see just how everything out front stayed so clean and tidy. These unpainted concrete walls were what the mall was really made of and on occasion, when they were putting in or taking out a new store, you could see where the unpainted met the paint and how the clean and modern was just a mask worn to entice and deceive the people who walked its floors.

I strolled around the food court, taking in the gap-toothed remnants of what was once one of the largest retail centers in the state. I walked to where my store had once been. The flexible steel grate was down and the darkened sign over the entrance read, "Motherhood Maternity." Strange. Strange that a maternity store could find itself among the elite.

Yes, there once was an elite group of retailers in the mall. I'm pretty sure it was something that happened in every mall, or at least the big ones. You see, certain companies got preferred real estate within the superstructure based on their overall appeal to the customers. There was a little strip of stores lining the inner wall between the food court and the escalators to the next level. Being in one of these spots was a big deal because nearly everyone who walked through the mall was forced to pass your store. It was an enviable place to be and although I don't know for a fact, the rumor was that the mall management would make potential tenants of, "The Mezzanine" perform all kinds of crazy, expensive, and sometimes even debasing tasks to be allowed into the most prime of prime real estate. It was hard for me to grasp how a maternity store would either be interested in or manage to win a spot in this coveted space. But the fact that it and the stores on either side of it were empty suggested that standards on occupancy had been relaxed since I'd roamed these halls with my name tag on.

I wandered down a little further, stopping in to a few of the remaining shops. Red, yellow, and orange Clearance and Closing signs were in every window and everywhere I went uninterested employees slouched and leaned, not bothering to reorganize or tidy up anymore. It was a depressing sight.

After about half an hour I came back around to the empty Motherhood store and stopped. I tossed my empty cup in the bin and sat on the bench across from the store front and reminisced. I thought of the day I'd asked my dad to borrow ten dollars and he gave me a lecture and a command that I go get a job. So, I rode my skateboard to the mall the next day after school and filled out applications. I must have just been lucky because when I brought my application back to Sam Goody, the manager looked over it and gave me an interview on the spot. The next day I was issued a black apron and a temporary name tag and started sorting compact discs and music books for six dollars an hour.

It had been a fun job, with lots of cool perks like employee discounting and discounted concert tickets. Sometimes touring bands would come in and drop off stacks of cassettes or seven-inch records to give away. The hours were easy and the people I worked with were friendly and fun. And working in a record store upped my apparent "cool" factor by a lot. It wasn't that I'd been bad with girls or anything, but once they found out I worked in a record store, they always seemed to pay a lot closer attention than before. It was the coolest thing to happen to a sixteen-year-old music fan like myself.

As my mind wandered, I stared at the store that I had looked forward to going to nearly every day for the year that I'd worked there. There used to be a little kiosk off to the side that made and sold gourmet popcorn. "Colonel Kernel's Perfect Pop." We had all agreed that it was the best popcorn ever made, and to this day, I've never tasted its rival. Off in the distance, the carousel kicked on again with its upbeat calliope music and for a moment I felt sick. How many children had ridden that thing on the best day of their lives? And I now had documents in my bag stating that due to excessive costs associated, the carousel would not be salvaged prior to demolition; it would be destroyed when the mall came down next year.

The circus music continued, and I glanced down the hall to where the toy store had once been. It was now some kind of cut-rate men's suit store, full of polyester separates. The pedestals on either side of the door, however, were unmistakable. When I was a kid, this was a Circus World toy store, later a Kay-Bee, and on the pedestal to the right stood the figure of the mascot Shruggs the Clown, and on the left, Huggs the Sea Lion, Shruggs' trusty sidekick, complete with ball on his nose. I remembered coming to the mall with my mom and grandmother so often and almost every time they would make me pose for pictures with Huggs and Shruggs. I think my mom has an entire album of those pictures. When I'd worked at the record store, Huggs still held vigil outside of the store, where Shruggs the Clown had been knocked over or broken some years before. Now, however, the stark overhead fluorescents reflected off shiny, cheap material and the only signs of those two ever-present mascots from my childhood were the raised and rounded platforms that now had gaudily dressed mannequins holding signs that said, "Everything Must Go!"

I shook my head and turned my gaze back to what used to be my record store. What a shame. So many memories, so many good days. So many bad days, for that matter. I remembered one Saturday when a clerk at the Gap got stabbed by her stalker right in front of a bunch of customers. I was taking out the trash when the assistant manager of the Taco Bell was shot in the parking lot in a botched robbery attempt. I shook my head and tried not to think about the time a three-year-old kid named Brian Charles climbed into the central fountain and somehow drowned in water that was only six inches deep.

Yes, it wasn't all sweetness and light. But to be fair, any population of people is going to have bad things happen from time to time. And yes, some horrific things happened, and yes, I was there to see them. But no matter what you think, no matter what your friend's cousin's girlfriend may have heard, all the rumors about cults and killers and kidnappers is not true. There is no group of phantom mall walkers, the fountain is not whispering, and the mall is not sinking. Or, at least, it wasn't when I and some of my coworkers started making up those stories around a campfire in my senior year of high school.

You see, we would know. We were in the mall after dark and sometimes late into the evening if we had to take inventory or something. We saw the fountains turned off each night, or during maintenance. Hang around a mall long enough, you get to know people and people like to talk about the weird culture that their particular place of employment represents. Add that to general mall culture and a bunch of heavily buzzed teenagers trying to impress one another, and you get the Haunted Tavistock where kids always go missing and...

Suddenly, I smelled popcorn. And not just any popcorn. No, this was Colonel Kernel's Perfect Pop somehow back from the dead! I realized it was impossible even as I was getting to my feet and trying to find the source of the smell. Colonel Kernel had used a special, vintage kind of popper that was rumored to have been used at an old traveling circus. They could make both small and large batches and whenever they did, the air all around that side of the mall smelled like pure heaven. And here it was again!

Was I asleep? Was I dreaming? Had I simply dozed off sitting on my bench in front of my old store? I, for one, didn't care. It didn't seem like a dream. Everything looked exactly as it had, calliope music playing, the echo of the fountain's rushing water, the canned jazz piping through the speakers high above... The only thing different was the nearly overpowering aroma of the best popcorn that anyone on Earth had ever made. I began to move toward the smell. An idea struck me: Maybe, just maybe, and this was a longshot but... What if Colonel Kernel had sold off or left their special popper behind? What if someone in one of the food court stalls was now using it? Did they know what they had? I needed to find this popper and its owner and offer him or her insane amounts of money for it and I needed to do it now.

I was almost to the stairs when I heard a panicked scream. I spun on my heels and ran toward the sound, as something was dreadfully wrong. I turned the corner and there on the floor in front of the Motherhood Maternity was a girl, curled up in the fetal position, screaming at the top of her lungs. And as if this wasn't a weird enough sight, people just passed by and let her scream. Some casually stepped over her but most ignored her altogether. This girl, she seemed to be about sixteen or seventeen, just lay there, body wracked by huge sobs, taking deep, choking breaths between screams, eyed wide, trembling, and totally lost. I slipped off my jacket and ran to her, covering her in it and telling her to calm down.

"Take it easy, Miss, I've got you." I said as I approached and tried to put my coat over her trembling shoulders. Her head snapped up and she stared at me with wild, searching eyes. No longer screaming she stared at me and said, "You can see me?"

"Uh, Miss-"

"CAN YOU SEE ME?" She screamed, her throat choking and slipping hoarse on the last word, "ANSWER ME!"

I stared at this strange girl for a second before nodding my head, "Yes, I can see you," I said, "Can you see me?"

She hopped to her feet and threw herself into me, wrapping me in a desperate embrace, "Oh thank GOD! You found me! I was so scared, and it's been so long! So dark! Is it over now? Was it some sort of a trick? I thought I was dead. I felt like I was gonna die so many times. But I always wake up right here and no one can ever see me! They just step over me like I'm not even there and the Man is always watching, and I can never get away and then... Now you're here and you saved me! Oh god, thank you! Finally."

"Listen, Miss. I'm not sure what's going on, but you look like you might need a doctor. Can you tell me your name?"

"It's Heather. Um, Quinlan. Heather."

"Okay, my name's Ken and I'm going to call somebody to help you, okay?"

"Okay."

I pulled out my phone to call 911 but there was no reception or Wi-Fi. "Weird. System must be down."

"What is that?" asked Heather.

"iPhone," I shrugged, "Just got it, in fact. Can't say I'm too impressed with it." I shook the phone a couple of times, hoping it would connect as Heather slumped to her knees, tears welling at the corners of her already swollen eyes.

"Oh no," she said meekly.

"What is it?"

"Mister Ken, I think I recognize you. You uh, used to work in the record store that used to be right there, didn't you?"

"I did," I nodded, still trying to get my phone to connect.

"I think I know why you can see me. We. We have to go. Now. He's coming for you."

"What do you mean? Go where? Who's coming?"

There was a whipping sound and Heather pushed me out of the way as something large flew within inches of my head and crashed into the window in front of me. It was a mannequin's arm and had been thrown with such force that it completely shattered the display glass at the front of the store. There was the snap-clank sound of a Zippo lighter being struck, and I caught a glimpse of a man in a suit and hat walking toward us.

"We have to go, NOW!" said Heather, pulling frantically on

my hand. I looked once more at the broken window and the plastic arm peppered with broken glass and it occurred to me, much slower than it should have, that someone had just tried to kill me. I turned with my strange new friend and we ran as fast as we could away from the food court and darkened Motherhood Maternity store with the smashed window.

We moved as fast as we could to the far end of the darkened Macy's wing. We made it to the escalators and took the steps two at a time, Heather holding my hand and dragging me along like a child. We got to the third level before we began to slow. But then the power on the escalator went out suddenly and we both lurched forward, almost losing our footing. At the bottom of the stairs stood the man in the black suit, in one hand he held the mannequin's arm he had thrown earlier. With the other, he casually brought a cigarette to his lips.

"Don't look at him. If he locks eyes with you, he's got you." Heather said as we moved onto the third level balcony. We jogged a bit, then she stopped and pulled open a security gate and rolled under it. "Come on, we can hide here for a while."

I dropped to my belly and rolled under the gate as she pushed it closed. We then moved to the back of the store and crouched behind the long-abandoned checkout counter. One of the columns was mirrored, so we could see the front of the store and I hoped that despite this, nobody could see us. We sat huddled for a while and I was just about ready to give up. What was this running for? Who was this girl? At any rate, we should just call mall security and tell them some unhinged person is throwing things at customers. I checked my phone again- no signal. I relaxed a bit and made as if to stand up, but Heather pulled me back and held me down. A second later, there was a clinking sound as the well-dressed man walked by, dragging the mannequin's hand across the links in the security gate.

He called, a deep authoritative voice soaked in malice and barely suppressed rage, "Dear Heather, I fear there's been a misunderstanding. It's not you I'm after. Not for a long, long time. You should know that," Something about that voice was far older than the man who employed it. There was an inflection there, proper English accented in a language that was dead long before English even existed—deep and primal, willing itself to be obeyed. Every hair on my body stood on end and I tried to suppress a shudder. "Your companion has some papers in his bag that will make all of us very, very *uncomfortable* if they leave the premises. I don't want to hurt anyone, I just need those documents!"

As I watched him pass, his eyes suddenly locked on mine through the mirror and he winked. He paused for a moment, then moved on, calling as he went, "Come on, my sweet Heather. I can make it worth your while. Just come out and let's have a talk, okay?"

His voice trailed off as he rounded the corner and Heather was on her feet pulling me further into the rear of the store. We went into and through what had been the stock room and then, as quietly as she could, Heather opened the large steel door that opened into the concrete hallway beyond. These corridors were brightly lit, despite the darkness of the mall proper. Years ago, these service corridors were crowded with delivery personnel and mall employees unloading stock and carrying trash to the compactors downstairs.

"He says he doesn't want to hurt anyone. That's a lie. He hurts people all the time. He enjoys it. If he gets angry, he'll reach into someone's chest and squeeze their heart, just to cause a commotion. He's lured children into the fountain before. One of them drowned. He... He's the reason I can't find my way out. It's him. It's all him."

"I'm sorry. Heather, is it? Please, just stop for a second."

"Not yet. Stay quiet until we are on the elevator with the doors closed. He doesn't come back here much. I think he avoids it because it's dirty. But that doesn't mean he can't come if he wants to."

We walked another several yards and then got into the elevator. Heather closed the outer and then the inner doors and pushed the button for the lower-level. We began our slow descent.

"What is going on, Heather? Why is that man chasing me? Why can't anyone see you but me?"

Heather looked at me sadly and shook her head. "I... I don't know who he is. All I know is that he's bad. Real bad. He's some kind of demon, or a ghost and he's been here, in the mall, for a really long time." She paused and wiped at her eyes. "I don't know what or how. I don't even know... I was just a stupid kid. I worked in The Gap on Level 3. All I remember is going to lunch one day and then, everything was different. Weird. The stores had different names, and everything was all mixed up.

I, like, slip. I slip through time. I go into the future and see things that don't make any sense. I also go backwards. I sometimes see my own parents, with me in the stroller pushing me around when I was a little girl. Sometimes I can control it, myself, what I see and do. Like now. Others, I'm barely here and I can feel myself fade. But I always wake up screaming on the floor out in front of that store you used to work at."

I listened to her story. I barely believed a word of it, other than she didn't have a clue what was going on. That was certainly true. This was ridiculous. I shook my head and prepared. When the elevator landed, I intended to run to the nearest exit, grab the nearest cab, shuttle, or bus, and get to the airport as fast as I could.

"There are others like me here too. There's a guy named Benjamin who appears occasionally. He thinks I'm stuck here like this because of how I died."

My head whipped around. Shocked I stuttered, "How you... "

"Died," she said. "I was about to go on lunch. Was going to stop by and talk to you, actually. I had the biggest crush on you back then, Kenney."

She smiled shyly, and I blushed. "I'm sorry, I don't remember that at all."

She shook her head, fresh tears welling up at the corners of her eyes, "You wouldn't have. I never got up the courage to say hello. I imagined it, of course. I imagined stopping in and making some small talk and you would... You would ask me out and I would say yes and we would live happily ever after." She hugged herself and shuddered.

"I had been getting these strange phone calls at night. Just weird breathing and hanging up. My parents called the police and we'd gotten a special phone with caller ID on it, you know? But it was an unknown number. Someone, either from work or from school was stalking me. I never knew who it was. I even slipped time once and watched it happen and I still don't know who it was."

"What happened, Heather?" I asked as calmly as I could. I could see she was on the edge of panic again and as the elevator set down I feared a full-on panic attack.

"He just walked up and stabbed me in the neck. Just like that. I don't even remember if it hurt or not. All I remember was, next thing I knew, I was talking to you and you were asking me out for lunch and I was the happiest girl in the world, and then everything started going wrong. I started seeing people burying themselves in the fountain. The mannequins move on their own sometimes. People wander around staring at some sort of light box in their hands like zombies. Then Benjamin and the others started showing up. I don't understand any of it. All I know is that the smoking man is part of it and that he's bad. And that I need to get you out of the building before he finds us again.

She pulled the latch and the doors to the freight elevator opened and we stepped onto a delivery landing next to a trash compactor. About a dozen mannequins lined the wall nearby, waiting for their turn to be crushed. Heather and I moved gingerly around them, as even in, or perhaps enhanced by the bright fluorescence, they looked quite creepy. As we got closer, *scritch scratch*, one of them seemed to move, causing others to fall.

"Run!" Heather said, and we were suddenly sprinting past the writhing, reaching hands of the dreadfully animated figures. If I didn't believe Heather was a ghost before, I could definitely believe it now. We rounded the corner and came to an entrance to the lower level. Just inside was where the movie theater had been, but it had been long closed and walled over. Now it was nothing but advertisements for the other stores in the mall. Heather and I crossed quickly as we moved back toward the food court.

"Why are we going this way? Why are we going back in?"

"Because he'll have those things at all the exits waiting. We have to get to a public area. He won't risk being exposed like that. Have to get you out a main door."

I sprinted as fast as I possibly could. I could see the light of the exit near where I'd come in hours before. The carousel was spinning and playing its music for another mob of nostalgia seekers. The area was quite crowded. I was going to make it. Then something crashed into me and everything went black.

*"Son? Son, can you hear me?"*

*I opened my eyes to an impossibly bright light. There were people all around me, but I couldn't make any of them out. They were just silhouettes against a painfully white background. My head. Oh god, did my head hurt. I tried to cooperate, to answer, to do anything, but instead I just lay back and put my arm across my eyes to shield them from the light.*

I thought of strokes and old-man physicals. Every fiber of my being screamed in pain. I have no idea what they hit me with but whatever it was had been heavy and it shattered when it hit my head. When the smoking man made himself known, I got to my feet and ran away as hard as I could. That's when I saw Heather, hugging her shoulders and crying, standing next to a tall, sad-faced gentleman. I ran to them and screamed, "Let's go! We've almost made it!"

Heather just looked and me and shook her head. "Oh, Kenney. I'm so sorry."

"Sorry for what? Let's go already! He's coming!"

I looked from her to the man, who only nodded at something behind me. I turned and stared as the crowd opened up. A young man in a black suit was yelling to the others to get back, that. "We're losing him!" He then knelt next to the body on the floor and began chest compressions and mouth-to-mouth. "Here, help me get this off him," he said as he slid the shoulder bag from the body. The man continued to press on my chest, unlit cigarette hanging from his lips the whole time. After a while, he glanced up at me and winked.

"What does this mean?" I asked, realization slowly dawning.

Heather was quiet, sobbing, shaking her head. The solemn man shook his head and said, "It means they've won again. The Manager will destroy the documents that sold and demolished the mall. Your company or another will send someone else, but they will encounter…. *resistance*, same as you. The building will close and fall into decay, but it will stand. I think that's all it wants.

"And who are you?"

"I'm sorry. I'm Benjamin."

"So, where did you work?"

"Me? Oh, I never worked here. I just appeared here one day. That is, I will appear here. About a year or two from now. I have… *penance* to serve. I haven't figured out how or why here yet. But I guess I've got a while longer to think about it."

He nodded to the crowd and we watched as the smoking man stood up from my cooling corpse, lit his cigarette, and carried my shoulder bag away from the scene. None of the bystanders either noticed nor seemed to care that I was being robbed and I wanted to say something.

But just then, I didn't really care either.

"Going to lunch, guys, see you in 30!"

"See you, Heather."

Heather's new shoes squeaked on the newly polished tile. She saw the cluster of shoppers lined up for the elevator. "One flight. How lazy can you be?" She thought as she weaved her way through the crowds to the stairs on the way down to the food court.

It was an unusually busy Saturday in the Tavistock Galleria, but nobody seemed to mind. This was commerce at its finest: happy shoppers with money to spend driving, parking, and waiting in lines to meet with clerks and salespeople happy to take it off them.

"Morning, Heather!" said a voice as she passed.

"Hey, Kenney," she said to the guy out in front of Sam Goody.

*"Don't be weird. Don't be weird. Don't be weird..."* she thought as she slowed down to talk to the tall, smiling teenager; his longish, *perfect* hair hanging in his eyes, "how's it going?"

Kenney shrugged and looked around, keeping his hands tucked in his company-issued black apron. "Kind of busy today. You?"

"Same. Gonna grab a bite. You wanna come?"

"Sure. Gimme a sec."

Heather crossed her arms and leaned on the support column that held up the balcony. She heard a noise and looked up to see some kind of commotion on the third floor. Mall security was running that way.

Kenney came back, apron and name tag stashed for the moment. "What's going on up there?"

"No idea. Probably another shoplifter. Not our problem. Shall we?"

"We shall."

He and she hooked arms and turned toward the food court. The carousel was running, and the festive circus music competed with the mall jazz and the fountains. The cacophony of happy shoppers filled the air as the pair wandered the hallway looking for something to eat.

"I don't know if I'm really in the mood for a full lunch," said Kenney, "But I could really go for some Colonel Kernel's if you'd like to share a bag with me."

"Nothing would make me happier," she said, "Let's go."

The pair turned back the way they had come toward the

gourmet popcorn kiosk. Both nodded at the smiling man in the black suit who appeared to be on his way to have a smoke. The man smiled back and snapped his Zippo, either unaware or in spite of the No Smoking sign on the wall right in front of him.

Kenney and Heather didn't notice and wouldn't have cared if they did. For them, nothing could ruin this one, perfect day.

# FAST FORWARD

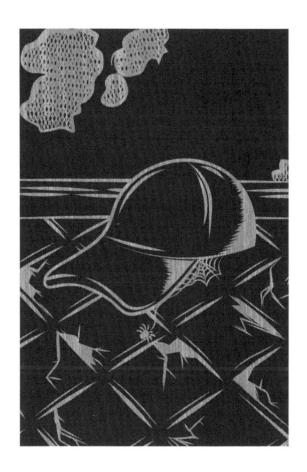

# FAST FORWARD

By Blair Daniels

TAVISTOCK GALLERIA DIDN'T LOOK ANYTHING LIKE THE MALL I remembered.

It was deserted. Empty. Gray. Where bustling stores once stood, there were now only dark cavities covered by silver grates. The space above each was stripped clean of signage, and I was left guessing what used to be there from the pins and faded marks.

I rounded the corner, straightening my cap. And there she was, sitting on a bench under one of the skylights.

Mellie.

*No. I can't do this.* I started to turn around—but it was too late.

"Jenny Reinhart!" She clapped her hands together and whooped. "I had half a mind you were standing me up!"

The memories came rushing back, unbidden. Calling me up, saying there wasn't a seat for me in the limo, an hour before the prom. Telling Chris Sonowski I had a boil on my back that looked like a volcano. She had always pretended to be my friend—but I don't think she ever really was.

"Yeah, it's me," I stuttered. *I can't do this, I can't do this, I can't –*

"Here's the necklace you wanted," she said, pulling out a thin, silver pendant. "Don't see why you're going through all this effort to get it back, though. It's not even pretty." She said the last bit in her classic, judgmental twang.

*Then why do I see you wearing it in half your Instagram pictures, Mellie? Why, for two years, is there always an excuses why I can't get my grandmother's necklace back?*

"Thanks, Mellie." *Okay, you got what you came for. Now leave.* "Anyway, I really should –"

"Hey, let's get on the merry-go-round. What do you say? For old time's sake."

Memories flashed through my mind. On that very same carousel–Mellie taking my Auntie Anne's pretzel. *You don't need the extra fat.* Mellie Running into another friend, and ignoring me the entire time. *Let's go to Starbucks, Carli. Oh, but Jenny can't come, she doesn't drink lattés.*

*No. Say no.*

"Uh, sure."

*Dammit! What's wrong with me?!*

We walked towards the kids' area. Past the flickering fluorescent lights, past the empty fountain, past signs saying EVERYTHING MUST GO. The only store that seemed to be doing well was *Hot Topic*, which was filled to the brim with emo kids trying on some clothes with snakes on them.

"Kids these days, huh?" I said to Mellie, attempting conversation.

She didn't reply.

"So... do you come back to West Mifflin a lot?"

Still no reply.

After what seemed like an eternity, the carousel came into view.

Crude statues of horses, painted with shiny lacquer, ran the perimeter. Mirrors and lights, bordered in cornflower blue and gold, adorned the interior wall. A jaunty rendition of *The Entertainer* played, its cheery tune clashing with the solemnity of the surrounding mall.

"Come on!" Mellie finally said, sliding a quarter in. It clinked deep within the machine, and the low rumble of a motor filled the room. We stepped onto the carousel—Mellie on the tiger, me on the gray horse ahead of it.

The lights along the inside of the carousel flickered. It began to turn, slowly.

"So, Mellie," I started, "What have you been up to?"

"Not much," her voice said behind me.

The carousel jolted.

AND THEN IT picked up speed. The mall outside began to spin, faster and faster, until it became a whirling mess of black and gray. *This thing goes faster than I remember,* I thought.

"This is *fun!*" Mellie squealed, her eyes shut tight.

The music sped up, until it was going faster than any human could perform. My hands grew slick against the bar; my body flew outwards. "Mellie?" I yelled, over the rushing wind. "I don't feel so good –"

The lights flickered.

Not the small, decorative lights of the carousel. The lights of the mall itself. Flickering, each time leaving a longer gap of darkness. "Jenny?" Mellie called—but her voice was small and frightened.

The cap flew off my head, whipping into the darkness.

And then –

*Crunch!*

The carousel rolled to a stop.

A silence filled the room. I slipped off the horse and leaned against the bar, waiting for the dizziness to stop.

"What was that?" Mellie groaned.

I peered out. Beyond the yellow halo of light surrounding the carousel, the mall was pitch black.

"Hello?" I called, stepping onto the carpet.

No reply, except for the echoes of my own voice.

Mellie stood up and brushed off her jeans. I pulled out my phone and turned on the flashlight. Lifting it high, I looked out into the mall.

It was empty. What few people had been in the mall were gone. And, somehow—maybe it was a trick of the light, or my nerves getting to me—it looked even more dilapidated than before. A crack ran down one of the support columns; the carpet was pocked with holes. And were those... *weeds* poking up through the floor?

"Hey. Did you drop this?" she asked.

She held up a red cap.

It was mine, all right. But it looked like it was twenty years old. The red coloring was bleached and faded, and it was covered in a thick layer of dust. *How did that happen?* I thought. *I just dropped it a minute ago...*

But wearing a nasty old cap was better than letting Mellie see my greasy hair, so I put it back on.

We walked down the hallway. "Do you think the carousel blew a fuse, or something?" I asked. "I mean, nobody's gotten on that thing in years, probably."

"But if it was just a fuse, the sky wouldn't be dark, too."

A chill coursed through my body, as I looked up at the skylights. *How is it dark already?* "This is going to sound crazy, but—do you think the carousel made us, like, time-travel? Like *Back to the Future?*"

She laughed. "Don't be ridiculous, Jenny." It echoed off the empty walls, making it sound like a chorus of people in the shadows of the mall was laughing with me.

Then I flared with anger. "Stop laughing at me," I snapped. "I know it sounded ridiculous, but this is a weird –"

"I'm not laughing *at* you," she replied. "I'm laughing *with* you."

"Doesn't feel like it." I turned to her, my eyes flaring. "You've always been mean to me, Mellie. And I used to think it was because there was something wrong with *me*. That I wasn't funny, or pretty, or cool. That I said dumb things I wasn't supposed to say." Heart racing, I leaned in.

"Now I know it isn't something wrong with me. It's something wrong with *you*."

She stared at me for a moment, her blue eyes wide.

But before she could respond –

A faint rustling, from the shadows behind us.

"Hello?" I called.

No reply.

"Let's get out of here," Mellie said, trying not to sound scared. But her darting eyes and quickened pace belied her tone.

"There's an exit upstairs, isn't there?"

We walked up to the escalator. It was still and dusty, as if it hadn't been used in years. I took a step onto the ridged, black metal; Mellie followed.

*Snap.*

"What's that?" Mellie asked, gripping the banister.

It sounded like plastic snapping, or wood splintering, or something hard falling to the floor. "I don't know," I replied. "Maybe the mall is just... settling?"

We climbed up the escalator. It groaned and creaked dangerously under our weight. As we got to the top floor, the flashlight fell on the entrance to the abandoned Macy's.

The blank faces of white, plastic mannequins stared at us, stripped clean of clothing.

"Left—it's on the left, isn't it?"

We ran down the hall, stumbling over broken beer bottles, pieces of garbage and dust. My hands fell on the handle; I pushed –

It didn't budge.

"They're locked," I whispered.

Mellie heaved her entire body weight against the door. It shook and rattled underneath her.

"Let us out!" she screamed, to no one.

"Maybe we can break the glass, or –"

A noise broke the silence.

*Thump, thump, thump.*

I whipped around and raised the phone.

At first, I didn't see anything but the broken bottles, the empty glass displays, glinting back at me. But then Mellie raised a trembling finger, and I saw it.

A dark shape, poking out of what used to be Hot Topic.

"Hello?" I called. "Hey, uh—the door's locked. Can you help us?"

"Jenny, they could be a murderer!" Mellie hissed. "Let's just break the glass and get out of here!"

But as soon as I turned—as soon as the flashlight's rays turned away from the hallway, leaving it in dark shadow—I heard it.

*Click, click, click.*

I raised the phone again.

A shadow, halfway between us and Hot Topic. Still as a statue, just standing in the middle of the hallway. My heart began to pound. Shaking, I took a step forward.

"Jenny, what are you doing?!"

As the shape got closer, I froze. Yellow, blank eyes. Black stripes rippling across its body. White fangs, poking out from under its jaw. Its body glistened oddly in the light, as if painted with something shiny.

It was a statue of a tiger.

That hadn't been there, a moment ago.

Mellie and I backed away.

As soon as the light receded—as soon as the tiger was again in the shadows—the clicking resumed.

*Click, click, click.*

We ran down the escalator. *Thump, thump!* I could feel the vibrations underneath my feet, feel the escalator shaking with its steps. I jumped the last few steps, out onto the carpeted floor.

*Click! Click! Click!*

We ran towards the carousel.

*Click!*

I shut the flimsy metal gate behind us.

*Click!*

"Put the quarter in, and let's go!"

"I don't have any more!"

"*What?!*"

"I don't." Her voice quavered, her lip trembled; it was the first time I had ever seen her cry. "I don't have it! And it's coming and –"

*Thump, thump, thump.* A shadow paced back and forth, just outside the halo of golden light spilling onto the carpet.

"Then how are we going to get back?!" I hid my head in my hands, but tears never came. Instead, my mind raced—*is there anything else we could use, anything like a quarter –*

The necklace.

With a shaking hand, I fished the thin chain out of my pocket.

Mellie looked at me with wide, terrified eyes. When she saw what I was about to do, her expression turned from fear to sadness. "Oh, Jenny. I'm… I'm so sorry."

With a *clink,* I put it in the machine.

The musical tones of *The Entertainer* began.

We climbed on. Before I could hoist myself up onto one of the horses, it jolted into motion. The *thumps* faded underneath the music, the rushing wind; the world outside became a blur of gray and black.

And then I slipped.

I opened my mouth to scream—but all that came out was a dry croak. I was falling, fast, away from the light of the carousel, towards the darkness of the mall. A warm gust of air on my neck, and I could almost *feel* the smooth, strange skin of the tiger…

And then a hand grabbed mine.

"I got you, Jenny!"

With a grunt, Mellie pulled me back up onto the carousel. We clung to each other, eyes shut tight, screaming like mad; but even so, I could tell the world around us was growing brighter, noisier.

*Crunch!*

The low hum of chatter and laughter filled my ears; the brightness of the skylights burned my eyes.

And then the carousel rolled to a stop.

Sunlight spilled in through the skylights. A few people turned to stare at us, then shrugged and continued their shopping. A child cried somewhere in the distance.

Mellie smiled—probably the first genuine smile I've ever gotten from her. I just stared at the carousel, blankly, tears threatening to roll down my cheeks.

But then I saw it.

"Mellie! Mellie, look!"

Where the tiger had stood, behind the gray horse –

There was now just a bare, golden pole, splintered in the center.

# RETAIL THERAPY

# RETAIL THERAPY

By Erin B. Lillis

I was standing in the dressing room again. It was the second time this week and since the mall is failing I kept thinking I could get in and out without anyone catching me in the throes of my retail therapy. But apparently not.

Three days ago, it was Yolanda from Weight Watchers and she came up on from me behind in the line at the Panda. I HAD been about to order a Beijing Beef combo but Yo was up on me like, "Denise! Hey honey! You about to use some cheat points too?" She laughed. I mirrored her in mirth and then ordered a Kids' Broccoli and Beef.

Yolonda leaned over my shoulder and asked the clerk, "Can I get her cookie?" before turning to me and adding, "You don't mind, right? I give them to my husband."

"No, it's fine," I lied and added to the clerk, "Yeah, can she have the cookie?"

"Yeah whatever. We're closing this month, so we just have

them all out at the end of the counter. Take as many as you want."

"Oh Lord save us!" Yolanda laughed and moved up to take my place in line.

"It's good that we're in this together, right?" I awkwardly attempted to fist bump Yolanda but just sort of knocked her lightly on the shoulder when she didn't raise her own fist. "I'll just go ahead and grab some cookies for your husband and totally none for myself."

Needless to say, I doubled back to the counter after I shook Yolanda and shoved two handfuls in my purse.

And now here I am in this dressing room at the Victoria's Secret, looking at my Spanx-saddled body from three angles thanks to the "heavenly" fluorescent bulbs that have shown me parts previously unknown to myself. *Annnnnd* to add insult to injury I can hear my ex mother-in-law in the dressing room next to me chatting on her cellphone.

Gloria. A Midwest Helen Mirren or Jessica Lange in her early 60s and not looking a day over 45. I'm sure her exquisite body is not a thing a daughter-in-law is supposed to notice but it was like a classical film scene whenever we'd visit and she'd open the door to her house. Rays of sunlight would spill through modern stained glass highlighting her statuesque frame as her hair flipped over her shoulder in slow-motion. I used to tell Grant, her son and my husband at the time, that I'd totally go gay for his mom. That generally resulted in two minutes of retching sounds as I laughed, and Gloria rushed to get her son water thinking I was some kind of sadist.

My respect for Gloria, however, was not mutual. She revealed her true colors pretty early on in our relationship. She never thought I was good enough for her son, so she kept pop quizzing me on shit in front of him to make me look dumb.

For example this one time when we were all in the market picking up Thanksgiving supplies she burst out with, "POP QUIZ - What is the capital of Denmark?" I bet you thought I was exaggerating. No, they were literally pop quizzes. *AND SHE GRADED THEM!*

"Um...Copenhagen I think," I answered, proud of myself.

"Easy ones first, of course. How about Slovenia?"

"Transylvania?"

"No. SLOVENIA. You should know the place as its named after you."

"Ha. Ha. Venia..zine?"

"Ljubljana. Hmph. How about Georgia?"

"Oooh I know - Atlanta!" I said with a little skip in my step.

"We're doing countries - I thought that was obvious."

"Oh ok. Oh wait."

"Clock's ticking."

"I actually know this. It's Tbilisi."

"Tbilisi. Right," she said disappointedly.

"Impressive. Why do you know that?", Grant asked me.

"I think it was like... on an episode of the MMC."

"The what?" Gloria asked, wrinkling her eyebrows in an uncharacteristic wrinkling of anything on her body.

"The...Mickey Mouse Club," I replied quietly aware of my own ridiculousness.

"Oooookay...learns from a mouse. Well that's 2 out of 3. So let's say 67%. That's hardly passing," she informed us while adding a bag of flour to our shared cart.

"That's HARDLY fair given that there were only 3 questions!" I argued.

"I'm calling it a fail."

"WHHAT?! ARE YOU KIDDING?! That's a D fucking plus!" I yelled in the aisle. Gloria put her hands to her ears for a second and then pivoted.

"Grant?? Sweetie?"

"Yes Mom?"

"You're dating a D+ student."

"We're MARRIED!" I laugh yelled back at her.

Turning back to me she mouthed, "For now."

Grant, in a moment of chivalry jumped in, "Mommmm leave her alone."

Gloria snarkily whispered over her shoulder as she rolled the cart around the end cap, "Just drop out."

"Ohhh no. I'm graduating at the TOP of this bitch!"

"Can you watch your language in public places?" Grant scolded.

"What are you? The po-po?" I countered as Grant rolled his eyes.

Grant never really did like those jokes... for Grant IS actually the po-po in this town. Or was. I kinda talked him into bringing home some of the unclaimed confiscated police property once and he did. And he got caught. And he lost his job. And he's now a mall security cop at the new mall across town. And Jesus Christ it was just a crock pot!

Well he blamed me and was too manly for couple's therapy because he could, "handle his own problems without bringing some stranger into it," and so long story short he's now my ex-Grant and I'm sure Gloria loves that.

And now I was stuck in these Spanx and was pretty sure this is how I was going to die - trapped in these human constrictors mere inches from my arch nemesis.

And then I noticed... IT. A skin-colored mole. On my back. I'd never seen it but then again, I'd never seen most of my body in that unholy glow before. I tried to angle in closer, leaning my shoulder down to the mirror closest to my right but when I did I made shadows in the wrong places. So, I twisted my body round and tried to look at the mole from the mirror in front of me reflecting the one behind me... that was the one reflecting the mole... you get it right? Anyway, so it was on the back of my right shoulder and I finally got the angle right but then I was too far away to see it clearly. So, I pulled my phone out of my purse and tried to reverse selfie it but the pictures just kept coming out too bright. Like one of those light leak filters... or I guess like a real light leak. Then my dumb phone just crashed altogether, and THIS WAS LIKE THE EIGHTEENTH TIME THIS HAS DONE THIS SINCE THE NEW OS UPDATE, APPLE!!!!

"Please keep it down," I heard from Gloria's stall.

Fuck... that was my outside voice.

Figuring it would be more awkward to not respond I attempted to disguise myself, "ARE YOU TALKING TO ME?"

"D Plus is that you?"

Trying to think quickly I responded, "I'M A TRIPLE D THANK YOU VERY MUCH," which I thought would definitely disguise me since I'm a B on a good day.

I suddenly heard the "ooooohhhh sexxay lady" part of Gangham Style. Shitfuckfuck... it's my ringtone for Gloria.

I tried to answer and whisper solemnly, "Uhm hello? I'm so sorry I'm at... a funeral and I have to whisper."

"I CAN HEAR YOU!" rang out from Gloria's dressing room.

"OK YEAH? WHAT? HELL!"

"Nothing. Just surprised to run into you here. Seems a little out of your budget."

"Oh yeah well there's a sale. Surprised you'd sink so low as to pay less than luxury prices."

"Well, I was just leaving anyway. The quality here has gone downhill."

"Go to the other mall. I'm sure Grant can point you to all of the high-end merchandise."

I heard her grab the handle with the force of her Pilates toned arm and turn it but there was no aggressively loud door swing. She didn't emerge. I heard her try again but nothing.

"Great. I think this door is jammed. It's no wonder this mall is going under. Maintenance has gotten lax all over this place."

"The mall is going under because of bad press. People keep reporting about all this spooky shit that keeps happening here. But I mean you probably saw all of that in your cauldron, right?"

Gloria took a moment to digest that and then I heard her huff and go for the door again. But again, no budge.

"Listen. I would like to do nothing more than issue one well-placed bitch slap on to your 'I wish you were still a virgin' cheek but I seem to be trapped at the moment."

Just then we both heard the high pitched and crackly voice of a third person in the dressing rooms slowly say, "Ladies, I've been trapped here for three days."

"Great. You do voices now. You can add that to your circus resume," Gloria shot at me.

"OK LISTEN... I took one aerial silks class BECAUSE I HAD A GROUPON!"

"I am not that other girl's voice," said the Zelda Rubinstein sounding person.

"Ma'am/Sir - what is it ever that you mean?" Gloria asks in her best sotto voce.

"I mean... I'm my own person."

"No, I mean, what do you mean that you've been trapped here for three days" Gloria responded.

"Oh. Well...I think this dressing room is a place between realities and I think we each have to face our own demons before we can be allowed to leave." The voice paused before continuing. "Or like maybe they closed the mall and forgot about us, I don't know. I ain't crazy, though."

While the crazy lady had been talking, I'd been unrolling myself from the Spanx and was trying to pull my pants back on when I noticed that mole again. Or rather, I noticed where it HAD been. But now it was gone. I kinda stood up fast and lost my balance, falling into the changing room wall. The three mirrors clattered on their plastic wall hooks as I slid to the floor.

"It sounds as though one of you has met your demon," the raw voice cracked out.

"No, my pants are just assholes," I informed her.

But now that I was on the floor, I had a new perspective. There'd definitely been a gap under the door when I came in but now when on the ground and expecting to see the paws of the stranger and the exquisite ankles of Gloria atop some designer heels under the door - there was just a beige 1980s department store looking "void." It was like a grey and beige checkerboard plaid that went on for seemingly miles. I thought voids were supposed to be ... void?

Then I caught the movement of something out of the corner of my eye and I turned the other direction. I leaned forward slightly and saw it, in the mirror across from me (which was reflecting the mirror behind me that reflected where the mole had been... let's not do this every time - there were three mirrors, they reflected things - you can connect the dots). It was a bump... but it was moving. It wasn't just moving... it was mobile. It was crawling from one side of my back to the other and then it started to appear as if it were bubbling and growing. I jumped up, untangled myself from the pant leg and tried to turn my back to the mirror again.

"The fuck is that?" I asked myself.

"What?" Gloria inquired.

"It's a bump. Or several bumps... or I don't know... It... They... They're moving."

"Bumps? Where?"

"On my back!"

"Great, STD-Plus! What did you give my son?!"

"Oh, get over yourself, Miss Fine and Mighty! Whatever this is ... it's NEW!"

"It's her demon," the mysterious person cracked out.

"Her ... demon?" Gloria let the second word roll in her mouth like she was trying it out for the first time.

"Woman! Rewind your mind. I JUST TOLD YOU THIS."

"OK TANGINA. The demon we each have to face. OK."

"Yours will come soon," the mystery person sing-songed.

"Yeah alright. Has anyone else tried their doors?"

Gloria rattled the door again and I could hear her putting all of her muscle into it but it still didn't budge. I reached out and tried my door too but found it equally unlockable.

"Ok Stranger. So, what do we do?" I bit.

"Does it seem like I know? I'VE BEEN TRAPPED HERE FOR THREE DAYS," Zelda proclaimed. To herself, she muttered, "Bitches don't listen."

Off in the other dressing room stall, Gloria was talking to herself about "these damn smart phones!" so I assumed she was trying to dial or text for help. If she was having the same problem I was she was seeing no bars, no WiFi and all the apps were frozen. When she gave up she started politely yelling and then really yelling for some help from the shop girls.

"Well what's YOUR demon at least?" I asked, trying to get a grip on our situation after Gloria's cries had resulted in no response from outside - as if, like our guide had suggested, we weren't quite wholly in our reality. I heard Zelda take a deep breath.

"When I first arrived, I was trying on a pair of yoga pants when I saw a shaggy white goat behind me in the mirror."

I imagined the miniscule Ms. Rubinstein as if in a flashback sequence, hazy with a dreamlike echo as she faced the animal.

"Oh, save me Jesus, it's White Philip!" The goat brayed and stomped a foot at Zelda.

"OK baby, back up. Back up," I told the goat in the reflection, but it reared, and I jumped. Knowing I wasn't going to get out of this without a confrontation, I slowly turned around to face the thing. And ... it wasn't there. I looked in the mirror again and the goat in it's white, furry glory, was back. But just behind me in the mirror... not really here in the real world. So, I avoided looking in the mirror and figured I'd just pay for the pants on the way out so I didn't have to waste time changing back and that's when I discovered I couldn't open the door."

"I cried out for help. I tried using my phone, but the screen was just ... white. Like light had leaked into it and it wouldn't respond to anything. I tried to crawl out under the stall but if you haven't noticed yet, it's like some sort of time warp beige endless nothing out there. I slid my torso out, but I was so... bored I had to pull myself back in here.

So, I spent the first day avoiding looking in the mirrors. I tried to dislodge them and turn them around but that just made the demon goat angry and he made a godawful racket all night. Middle of what I think was yesterday I cracked and turned the mirrors around again.

I wasn't prepared..."

"Oh, what the hell is that?" Gloria interjected.

"It was a dramatic pause," the disembodied voice replied.

"No, not you. There's some kind of creature in here. I think."

"Your demon," the voice said ominously.

"Looks more like small rodent."

I heard the shuffle of Gloria's polyester and rayon blend move to the corner of her dressing room as she investigated.

"Shoo Shoo!! Oh, where the hell did it go?"

"It's in the mirrors," Zelda advised.

"No, I think it's in this "Thank You Thank You Thank You" bag...SEE! What'd I tell you. Bad maintenance in this place."

It sounded then as if Gloria had picked up her notoriously large handbag and started swinging it at a corner of the stall.

"SHOO!! SHOO!!!"

"Ladysir... I'm not sure if what you're saying is ... coherent but I think you're right about the mirrors. I'm seeing all these weird things on my body but they're only in the reflections," I reported to our wise consultant.

It was true too. The ripplings I saw moving across my back had traversed to the front of my body, according to the mirror, but when I looked down I just saw my own cookie-loving bod. Nothing that wasn't normally alarming. But as I turned slowly around my whole chest was a living roiling entity in the reflections. Now if you'll recall, I took the compression garments I was trying on, off. And I fell out of my pants, so I was basically just standing there in my chonies staring at this canvas of flesh undulating until I began to see recognizable shapes appear.

"Ohhhhhhkay... this is not happening. This is some kind of fucked up Augmented Reality VR hoo doo and someone's trying to YouTube prank me, right? That unprofesh sort where you end up psychologically scarring people for life in the name of the Channel? This is not how you become an influencer, guys!"

No one responded to my slapdash challenge.

"WHERE DID THAT FUCKING THING GO?" Gloria yelled in the middle of a barrage of swinging and crashing noises.

"Listen to our friend here, Gloria! Look in the mirrors!"

Gloria gave a short burst "OOHHoooHHOOOHHH".

"Told ya," the voice and I chorused.

Meanwhile I stared aghast as the shapes in my chest rippled and coagulated into what looked like a small well-manicured hand.

"OK that was weird. It's like tiny Exorcist in here," I said more to myself than to my two companions.

I could hear Gloria rhythmically yelping now.

"Ouch! Shoo!! AHH! GET OFF!! AhhhOuch!" echoed from her corner of the room along with the sounds of glass banging, lipsticks and granola bars tumbling out of her handbag and hangers of discarded lingerie rattling about.

The coursing waves of my chest turned and twisted into now TWO tiny manicured hands that seemed to appear and disappear in time with Gloria's screams. It dawned on me that they were like a jerky flesh animation of two arms swatting at something.

. . .

"WHAT'S YOUR POISON?" yelled the voice at Gloria.

"Is it spiders? Mosquitos?" I added.

"It's. DAMN YOU. OW! One little..." her words suddenly came out choked as if she was deep throating one of the food court corndogs...she gagged and spit. "SPARROW!"

"Like a bird?"

"Yes, Nelly Furtado! A GODDAMNED BIRD." More vigorous swatting and swinging could be heard. "It keeps pecking at me!"

My chest flesh waved and stretched until it looked as though I was a funhouse mirror blob made of pale and freckly liquid mercury. The shape of a foot emerged from my neck, the toes spreading and cracking just under my chin as if I were a pair of fresh pantyhose and then it slid around the back of my neck. It was followed shortly thereafter by another. Then the gelatinous version of me formed full size legs extending from my shoulder blades like leg-wings. I was both horrified and impressed by the detail in the reflections.

Gloria screamed viciously again.

"That little shitwhistler just took my eye! Why IS NO ONE HELPING US??!"

She cried some more. I could hear her rocking and moaning.

"Look your demon in the eyes and understand each other," the voice uttered.

"THIS P.O.S. JUST STOLE MY EYE. It is CLEARLY NOT INTERESTED IN A STARING CON..." we heard another sudden choke and a liquid splutter. "It's cut my jugular," Gloria eeked out. "You understand what that means D Plus?"

"Burrrrn," Zelda whispered from her stall.

"I understand you should probably be quieter then," I retorted.

I looked at my hideous new form in the mirrors. A new set of pert designer boobs had emerged just over my existing broken-underwire-bra-clad ones... making my chest look like two semicolons next to each other. Two excess ear shapes nestled in the pillows of my eye bags, making me look even more like a sad clown. The tiny adult arms took turns emerging from my belly to gesticulate whenever Gloria moved. And those leg-wing things stretched and flexed showing off how limber they were. I realized I'd recognize those calves anywhere! Those were Gloria's chiseled calves!

What really confused me, though, was that my body had completely reformed into this monstrous new shape. I should have felt the skin ripping from the tendons and tissue as everything changed and grew. This should have been an excruciating transformation, but I didn't feel anything.

"I don't get it," I said aloud.

"Not surprised," Gloria said in a faint whisper.

"Shut up, no. I'm seeing all sorts of crazy shit over here and it SHOULD BE painful, but I don't feel it. Meanwhile Gloria's all "My eye! My eye!" and doing some kind of reenactment of The Birds in her stall. So why is my demon just visually torturing me?"

"You really wanna push it?" the wise voice wisely asked.

"What happened to you? Do you feel stuff?" I asked Zelda.

I heard the voice clear some of her rasp before she began.

"When I stood at the center of where the reflections of the three mirrors met - I held the gaze of the goat demon and his shaggy hair began to grow and grow. It came out and off of him like waves of water ...if it were made of hair and began to fill the changing room. I risked a peek around to see if the real stall was filling with the hair, but the goat hoarsely screamed, and I snapped my head back and watched.

I tried to close my eyes and shut the vision out, but the goat would scream and then I would scream. I tried to cover my ears, so I wouldn't have to hear the slippery sounds of the goat hair entwining and matting... but the goat would scream. I tried to focus my attention to other parts of my body to psychologically blind myself and still the goat knew and screamed louder. So, I was forced to watch, consciously, as I saw myself and began to believe myself surrounded, encircled, and ensnared by the goat fur from the silent but drooling beast that stood behind me and stared.

I began to panic and hyperventilate as I thought the snowy, soft hair of the goat might very well drown me, but the goat saw my rising terror and paused. I thought he'd stopped. I thought this was the end of it. But then it seemed the goat smiled as a tentacle of his hair stood before me and then gently pushed on my chest until I fell back into a cloud-like bed of his hair. It then grew over my eyes and I ... sorta fell asleep."

"You fell ASLEEP?" Gloria and I yelped together.

"I mean... it's comfy."

"So you've been like that for three days? How have you gone to the bath... no, nevermind," I spit out before realizing I didn't want to know the answer.

Gloria started screaming and spluttering just then again. But I realized that in all of her struggles I never actually heard a bird. If there were a real one, surely, we would have heard wings, whistles or something. But there was just Gloria's array of gurgles and gasps.

"Once you face your demon and accept him, you too can rest in his arms," the voice advised.

"The goat had arms too?!"

"It's a figure of speech! Hair! Wings.. whatever."

"So, you can feel the goat fur?" I asked the voice.

"Again, it's more like hair but yes. I'm lying in it right now."

"And Gloria can obviously feel the bird attacking her. So why can't I feel anything? You think maybe it's because I don't want to believe it?"

I heard the lock on the door turn slightly. I was onto something. I tried the knob, but it wouldn't open so I tried thinking out loud again.

"I don't want to believe that..."

Then something clicked in my head. Maybe it was because I'd switched over into Gloria's Pop Quiz adrenaline terror mode or maybe I'm just ... OK I'm like really good at making puns as a form of torture and the word play just hit me.

"I think I get it. Mine, I mean," I announced.

"Your demon?" the voice queried.

"No, I don't think it's a demon. I think... it's a metaphor."

"What?" Gloria and the voice chimed.

"So, hi, I didn't tell you my thing yet. Basically, those moving bumps I told you about before. They kinda formed hands and feet and... stuff... and I recognize the parts... they're Gloria's parts."

"Who is Gloria?" the voice asked.

"The bitch getting apparently eaten by a bird."

"My... parts?" Gloria whimpered.

"Yeah and every time you did something annoying over there, it got worse and grew more... Gloria. Do you get it?"

"Sorry, not following," the voice said.

"Gloria's getting under my skin!"

My skin began to ripple again. The leg wings sucked back into my shoulders. The hands melted into my neckline. The breasts, sadly, also disappeared but they were replaced by a face over my breastbone. Gloria's. It mouthed in a mock version of her voice.

"I thought you were tougher than that. You always seemed so strong."

I mustered up some confidence and announced to Skin Gloria and Real Gloria and the World, "Yes, Gloria. I didn't want to believe it...but your words hurt and stung and dug into me like thorns." I was on a little bit of a weepy roll then. "I let your poison seep into me. I tried to put up a wall but you poked and prodded and YES... I LET YOU GET UNDER MY SKIN. ARE YOU HAPPY NOW?!?"

The skin version of Gloria smiled, I think. And then dissolved back into my flesh. And the latch on the door to the dressing room turned and the door fell open. I wiped away tears and shouted.

"THAT'S IT GUYS. It's like a dream. You have to interpret it. You have to ... Self Help-Yourself?"

"I can't. I'm dying," Gloria managed to breathe out as if she'd bled completely dry already.

"I think I get it... so a bird in the hand is worth two in the bush? Sparrow... rhymes with arrow? Kill two birds with one stone..." the voice prattled.

"Is there more than one bird?" I asked Gloria.

"It's eating...me," she answered.

"OH. OH. OH! SOMETHING'S EATING AT YOU. IS SOMETHING EATING AT YOU? IS SOMETHING EATING AT YOU?" I yelled excitedly.

Gloria's breathing steadied. We could hear that, even as I, possibly cold-heartedly put my clothes back on while she was supposedly dying.

She began to clear her throat. I quietly zipped my jeans.

"Ahem.. ahm... that seems to be it. The wounds stopped

bleeding. The sparrow ...landed and is now just looking at me."

"OK more to do then. Do you know what it is ... that's eating at you?"

"Yes."

"I think you have to say it out loud. Or to the mirror or something. Like the other girl did," Zelda wisely concluded.

"Yes. OK. Umm. D Plus... I mean... Denise. I. Um... miss you."

"I'm sorry, what?" I choked out.

"I MISS YOU, OK. You were the only one of Grant's girlfriends..."

"WE. WERE. MARRIED."

"GIRLFRIENDS who became a wife that gave my sass back to me. Or anyone, for that matter. I ... respected you. I enjoyed your company. And I'm sorry and I regret ... that it may have been my vitriol that poisoned your relationship with my son."

Her door unlocked and swung open. She sat, defeated, on the dressing room stool that faced the three magical mirrors. Her head rose from her chest and we met each other's eyes and had a moment. I ran in and hugged her, and I admit there were a few tears. I may have also caressed her strong back a little but that's a different type of story.

"Ahem... a little help here," Zelda interrupted.

"White goats with long hair are the variety that make the wool for cashmere. You said you're just laying on a bed of this hair and it's just grown over your eyes, right?" Gloria took the lead.

"Yeah."

"And so..." Gloria circled her hand as she tried to coax the understanding out of the air.

"The...Cashmere..."

"The wool..." Gloria corrected.

"THE WOOL IS OVER MY EYES!"

There was a loud clatterthump then. My guess is that the bed of hair must have disappeared, and our advisor must have fallen to the floor. We heard her yell from the ground.

"OK HOW WAS I SUPPOSED TO KNOW CASHMERE COMES FROM GOATS?! THAT IS NOT EVERYDAY KNOWLEDGE!"

"OK well... do you think the wool is over your eyes somehow??"

"Well I don't think this Going Out of Business Sale is as big of a discount as they say it is?"

Her dressing room door unlatched, and the door swung open revealing... Yolanda.

"OH, COME ON!! I have been here for THREE DAYS! FOR THAT?!"

"Yolanda!?"

"Denise?! Oh, thank god you gave me your fortune cookies the other day. I was rationing them."

I grabbed the items I was going to purchase, and the arm of Gloria and we exited the store. Past the knowing eyes of the Angels that modeled the underwear we'd come to try on in the first place.

"Aren't you glad this brain o'mine was on the case?" I tapped my forehead and lifted an eyebrow at Gloria.

"You got two out three. 67%. D plus."

"FUUCCCKKK What is it with you?!"

# BITCHCRAFT

# BITCHCRAFT

By Samantha Mayotte

"Now introducing the Witchcraft Cult clothing line." Shelby read the sign with an eye roll. "Can you believe this store is still trying to be relevant? Like, it's not the nineties anymore. No one wants your weird goth clothes."

My girlfriend and I stood outside a popular goth store in the Tavistock Galleria, my town's local and slowly dying mall. She was dressed in a bright, happy pastel tee and a pair of designer jeans. She didn't realize that half my wardrobe came from that store. And I wasn't just talking "back in the day." The clothing line she was having a chuckle at had some of the most comfortable clothes to ever touch my body. Almost every article had this cool, creepy, snake creature on it. For the sake of not starting an argument, though, I didn't enlighten her on my personal feelings on the matter.

My opinions aside, I had to admit that she had a good point. With the influx of smaller shops coming in, including some pretty stiff competition in the supposedly alternative culture, it was hard to believe this store was still open. "Oh, Shel," I shrugged before seeing the other sign, "Hey! They're hiring! Hold on a second."

I was nineteen, still living with my parents while I went to community college. I could use the extra money to help pay for next semester's books, and maybe do something nice for my girlfriend. Most of our time together was just hanging out at the mall, window shopping in the same stores that have always been there, or hanging out at one of our family's houses.

She rolled her eyes at me for showing interest in their *Now Hiring—Inquire Within!* sign, but she gave me a smile and wandered off to a nearby jewelry kiosk to browse. I walked in, looking at an assortment of superhero and television apparel that lined the front of the store.

"Hi, can I help you find anything?" The overly cheery voice came from behind a body jewelry display case.

"Uh, yeah, I was actually trying to find someone to ask about getting an application?" I raised my voice to be heard over pop-punk music playing over the speakers.

A short young lady who could have been any age between fifteen and twenty-three popped out from behind the case, her blond hair sporting faded streaks of a rainbow's worth of colors. Her multiple facial piercings gleamed with the bright lights that shone in from the black arches I'd come through.

"That would be me, give me two seconds." The case creaked as she ran into it trying to maneuver around it, and after a few seconds and a muttered curse, she held her hand out to me. "I'm Constance, the manager."

I gave her hand a shake. "Avery. Nice to meet you," I smiled back, trying to mask my nervousness. At least here I knew that my labret ring and my tattoos wouldn't be an issue.

"Come with me over to the counter, I'll grab you an application." I followed her through the maze of shelves to the small countertop in the middle of the store that held the POS systems. "Actually, I'm sort of lying. We had a girl...quit, really unexpectedly, so we really need someone who can start like, immediately." Her chipper voice wasn't what I usually associated this store with, but it wasn't like you needed a certain type of speech pattern to enjoy dark clothes and heavy music.

"Oh really? I can start as early as tomorrow night. I have classes until–"

"Student?" she cut me off. I nodded. "Okay, perfect. We need someone to work the closing shift anyway. Do you have any nights that you wouldn't be able to work from five o'clock on?" I shook my head, trying to keep the hope out of my eyes. I could really use this job. "Awesome, this keeps getting better and better. Avery, you might just be my savior."

I gave a nervous chuckle as she continued. "Okay, so...what I'm going to have you do is, well, can you come in at like, three o'clock tomorrow afternoon?"

"Yeah, I can be here."

"Okay, great. It's not going to be a super formal initiation —oh my god no, *orientation* is the word I want. If you're a little late, no one's going to fire you or anything; if anything comes up and you're going to be *super* late, give me a call." She pulled a card from behind the counter and handed it to me. I pocketed it and went back to listening. "Dress code is, well, what you're wearing now is fine, so anything like that. We need two forms of ID, you'll have to fill out some tax forms - you've had a job before, right, you know the drill?" She shot me another smile and a small nervous laugh.

I chuckled. "Yeah, I'll make sure I have everything with me tomorrow."

Shelby was waiting for me underneath the dark archway when I reached the exit. "Flirting with another woman, I see," she said, clearly kidding.

I gave her a quick kiss on the mouth and we continued walking. "Hey, say what you want, but I've got myself a job. Maybe now I can take you out to a nice dinner once in a while."

"Alright, Avery, you can head out," Constance said, walking into the back room, where I'd been organizing the inventory.

After a few seconds of explaining how far I'd gotten in my endeavor, I took off my name badge and put in my back pocket as I headed through the store. It seemed like every store inside the Galleria was going through a dry spell. It was sad to see something that was once thriving fall to the age of internet shopping and Amazon Prime. I'd only been working there a few months, but I'd grown up in the area. I remembered when my parents used to bring me with them and how big and exciting it was running from store to store and throwing pennies into the fountain like it was a wishing well.

I was about halfway to the exit, passing by the old carousel, smiling at the peaceful, happy memories it stirred up, when I realized I'd forgotten my keys. I muttered a curse as I turned around and jogged back. The store was dark, but the metal security gate hadn't been pulled down yet. I guess it was my lucky night.

I headed around to the POS system and grabbed my keys

from the drawer under the register. There was a noise coming from the stock room, and I turned my head toward it, trying to place the sound. I told myself it was none of my business. I told myself that Constance was probably just listening to some new-age music while finishing up and there was nothing that I needed to go out back and check on.

Then I promptly ignored myself and crept toward the 'Employees Only' door.

Two steps forward told me it wasn't music, but I held onto my excuse like a life raft and kept going. Those were definitely real voices, and they sounded like they were chanting. It didn't seem to be English. Was it Latin? The more I listened, the more I realized that I had no idea what Latin sounded like outside of *The Exorcist*.

I don't know why I didn't just mind my own damn business and go home. If I'd just left, I could have gone to work for a few months, made some money, maybe even manage to save enough for next semester's books.

Instead, my dumb ass cracked open the door and peered inside.

What I didn't see was the picture most would assume, given the chanting I heard—black robes with big open hoods that covered everyone's faces and some Satanic symbol or pentagram carved or painted onto the floor.

Yeah, there wasn't any of that.

There were... A lot of employees from various stores in the mall, surrounded by a few boxes of inventory, and a few wall-hangings from the Witchcraft Cult line. Some of the chanters still wore lanyards with their name badges attached. What they were chanting wasn't nearly as important as what they appeared to be chanting to.

The employees were not standing around a painted pentagram, nor were they anywhere near a statue of Baphomet or Lucifer. Their eyes were closed, at least from what I could see, but something was obfuscating the far side of the room. It looked like pure darkness. It wasn't a shadow, but a wall of solidifying blackness. I gaped in growing horror as it took shape. Whatever it was, it was enormous. It seemed to be a giant…snake…person?

About four seconds later, it didn't much matter what it was or how massive. As I was crouching by the open door, paralyzed by my curiosity, the giant shadow's eyes—black pits with a blood red drop of color where the pupil should have been—looked directly at me. My own eyes widened, and it was all I could do to keep the urine *inside* my body as fear dug its icy claws into me.

My mind was tripping over itself trying to figure out what was I was seeing, while at the same time screaming at me to turn around, to get out of the store, out of the mall, to never mention what I'd seen to anyone and to just *get out*.

I was even going to do it—turn around and walk away, I mean. I hadn't quite forced my body to move yet when, of course, my phone chimed in my pocket; making a quiet, quick escape impossible. My hand raced to my pocket to try and turn off the ringer. *Son of a motherfuck*, I thought, finally silencing the thing. I looked up quickly from my phone, realizing it was too late to run.

The chanting had stopped, and all eyes were on me. Well, every pair of human eyes, anyway. The shadow's red eyes were nowhere to be found. At a loss for what to do, and without a good explanation for why I was crouched in front of the door, I smiled and waved, "Helloooo!" In an awkward, sing-song sort of way. I stood and backed away from the door just as Constance came through. She looked farther from happy than I'd ever seen her before, and I swear I could feel my heart jump into my throat.

"I get it, I think," I stammered, "This is some sort of, like, promo for Witchcraft Cult huh? It's pretty, um, awesome. And, like…" I could see that stalling was getting me nowhere, so I took a step back as I cried, "I didn't see anything! I don't even know any of you!"

She held up a hand, silencing my excuses. I was quite grateful for it. My heart was still pounding, and my babbling was probably due to the image of those red eyes boring into me.

"Okay, full disclosure: I forgot my keys." As if I had to prove it to her, I pulled them from my pocket and held them up to her. "Then I just…let curiosity get the best of me."

She smiled. *"There's* that honesty that I hired you for." The smile faded from her face as quickly as it had come. "Of course, now there's the issue of what to do with you." Constance shrugged, looking at the door to the back room. I didn't dare follow her gaze; my curiosity had gotten me into more than enough trouble already tonight. "Can't really have you going and telling anyone what you saw, can I?"

"To be fair," I tried, "I have no idea what I actually *did* see." It wasn't a lie, despite my shaking voice. I couldn't have explained what that…*shadow* had been. I was becoming more certain with each moment that it had somehow been a figment of my imagination.

Constance narrowed her eyes, but the intensity of her blue stare was nothing compared to those horrifying red ones. I felt other eyes on me, probably the crowd from the stockroom coming to see what my fate would be.

"Alright, go home." She said. I didn't let myself breathe a sigh of relief. I knew I wasn't out of the water yet. "I'll figure out what to do with you tomorrow. Until then, don't say a word about what you saw. To *anyone*, Avery."

I swallowed, trying to remember how to speak. Leave it to my stupid curiosity to get me caught up in some potentially life-threatening bullshit. I agreed not to say anything and headed out the door. I took out my phone and sent Shelby a text. We were supposed to hang out, and I had to come up with a damn good reason for why I was so late.

*I was standing by the door to the stock room. Everything was quiet, no more vaguely ominous chanting, just an overpowering, suffocating silence. The store behind me was a wall of darkness. The lights from the mall proper offered enough light for me to make out the security gate blocking the main exit. The only way out was through the back.*

*My hand was on the doorknob, but I couldn't make myself turn it. I could feel my heart racing in my chest. The anxiety from standing in the near blackness was starting to build, and I had to do something before the silence crushed me.*

*And oh man, do I wish I hadn't opened that door.*

*All I could see in the darkness of the room were those glowing red pupils. The room hadn't been breathing, but the thing inside it had been, and for whatever reason, it had set its sights directly on me.*

When I came in for work the next evening, still freaked out from my dream the night before, I couldn't help the rolling anxiety in my gut. I hadn't been able to shake the feeling that I'd been watched all night.

I'd thought about skipping town. Leaving. Never to be seen again. But I had no money, and I didn't think my parents would take too kindly to me stealing their car. I also hate to admit that I was just too afraid of what would happen to me if I didn't show up to work. I liked having money in my pocket, and if I could convince myself that everything that I'd seen had just been a dream, maybe things would eventually go back to normal.

It was busy, and I spent my first hour slaving over one of the POS machines, ringing order after order until the numbers bled together. When the last person finally did walk away with their bags, I rubbed my eyes and tried to stop seeing the numbers that had burned themselves into my corneas. I walked around, trying to organize the chaos that had happened during the rush and hoping I could keep myself out of the tiny, cramped box for at least a few minutes.

As the night wore on, I felt myself getting more out of it, mentally speaking. I felt out of tune with my own body, with my own mind. I couldn't wait to get out of work, so I could go home and sleep off whatever I was coming down with.

Five minutes before closing, I looked around, realizing that the assistant manager—the only person who had keys to the store—had disappeared. Thinking back, I hadn't seen her in nearly an hour. A voice I shouldn't have heard broke through the fog in my mind, its chipper tones sending a shiver down my spine. "Avery, can I see you in the back for a second?"

I turned to see Constance standing there, twirling her keys in her hand.

"Uh, yeah, I'll be right there." I felt my bones turn to liquid as I forced myself to move forward. Her words from the night before rushed back into my brain, and I worried what was going to happen to me.

I made my way back to the stock room and saw it arranged much like it had been the night before, sans the chanting crowd. Sitting idly on an opened box of merchandise, though, was my girlfriend.

"Shel, what are you doing here?" Something overcame my building fear, and I was suddenly more concerned for her safety than I could have been for my own.

"We're here to talk about you, Mr. Nosey-pants," Constance said, drawing my attention back to her. She smiled, but there was nothing warm or reassuring about it. "We're here because you got too curious for your own good and now you're in *way* over your head."

I looked to Shelby, who simply nodded at me as though she were in on some secret I was still in the dark about. "Over my head? Constance, like I said, I forgot my keys. I don't even know what I saw."

"Avery, it's not about what you saw anymore. It's about what saw *you*." I hadn't expected Shelby to chime in, but she had. How did she know what happened last night?

It was then that I really looked at her. She was wearing a dress from the Witchcraft Cult line that she'd once made fun of. I followed the white snaking pattern that ended in two red eyes on the collar of her dress. Those red eyes…were just like the ones I saw a few feet away from where I was standing. The same ones I'd seen in my dreams. What did the clothing line have to do with what I'd seen the night before?

"Don't worry, it likes you," Constance said with a forced giggle, but I certainly was worried. *What* liked me? She seemed to see my confusion and her laugh then was genuine.

"I really can't believe you haven't pieced it together. You've been selling the merch since you started working here."

I looked at Shelby's dress again, trying not to shudder at the two red jeweled eyes staring at me from her dress.

"The...snake? From the Witchcraft line?"

Constance had no expression as she nodded. "Not a snake, per se, but we can go with that. The reason that you're still here is because he picked you. I was thinking about having you killed, but you managed to keep your mouth shut."

"I never thought that *my boyfriend* would ever get such an honor," Shelby gushed. She was nearly bubbling over with excitement, but I caught the angry look she shot Constance at the mention of my potential assassination.

"Okay, so... give me a minute, here. We're selling shit with a giant demon snake - unless I saw something else last night - that wants me for some incredibly specific reason that I don't know about?" I'd seen enough horror movies to make a half-decent guess what a demon might want me for, but I wasn't about to press my luck and start making assumptions.

"You're not a sacrifice, babe, so stop looking at us like we're gonna stab you," Shelby said. She stood up from the box she'd been sitting on and her heels clicked on the concrete floor as she made her way over to me.

Constance huffed, rolling her eyes as Shelby enveloped me in a hug. "Shel, how did you even...I mean, when you first saw this stuff, you couldn't *stand* it. How are you now so... involved?"

She gave me a quick kiss but didn't answer my question.

"It's really an honor, Avery. I mean, think about it. You'll be co-inhabiting your body with a demon god. You'll have *everything* you could want."

"Uhhhh, what?" I'd be sharing my body with a what now? I

realized that I didn't have nearly as many answers as I wanted, and so many of my questions were being avoided instead of answered. "Okay, what in the fuck is going on? Someone has to start answering my questions or I'm seriously going to lose it."

Shelby gave my arm a loving squeeze. "Avery, relax. I've been meaning to introduce you to the Nest for a while. I was born into it. It's like a religion. Except that we just happen to know that our god truly *does* exist. And we've been working toward resurrecting the great *Naga* since before my grandfather was born. We're getting so close, and the other day when he saw you peeking in from outside during the hosting ritual, well, we found his host!"

She was overjoyed. I realized then that I didn't know my girlfriend nearly as well as I thought I did.

"And am I just supposed to be okay with all of this?" I asked. I was practically shaking with anger. Where was my choice in all of this?

"Yeah," Constance answered, startling me. She'd gotten so quiet over the past minute I'd nearly forgotten she was there.

"We've already started the preparations. Go home and rest, Avery. Come to terms with all this. We'll let you know when everything is ready."

IT FELT like I was coming down with the flu, so I confined myself to my room and gave myself an abundance of cold medicine for the next few days. Nothing seemed to touch it. Every waking moment I felt disconnected, like someone had stuffed my head full of cotton. I was sleeping more, and my dreams were becoming more unsettling. It never occurred to me at the time that the 'preparations' that Constance had talked about might have involved what was going on inside my own mind.

What used to simply be a shadow and a pair of eyes when I fell asleep was becoming clearer with every nap I took. Black scales covered the horrible reptilian body that slithered across the floor of the stock room. The scales gave way to smoother skin and a humanoid chest, though no less black. Two arms came out from a pair of broad shoulders, and a neck, and finally, a horrifying, black-as-night face. From its open maw two fangs emerged, dripping with venom. There was a flattened patch of skin that mimicked a human nose slightly below those black eyes, their red pupils burning into me.

I could hear it speaking to me, but not in any language I understood. It spoke whatever they had been chanting in the stock room, the one with too many vowels that wasn't Latin. It seemed to be...beckoning me, calling to me, telling me to come closer to it. As the days passed and as I felt sicker, it got harder to ignore, and a little more solid. Every time I sank into the dream I seemed to wake up a little closer to it. I didn't feel right calling it a "he" though it appeared to have masculine features. Although, I didn't know much about snakes, and since it became a snake just after its torso like some kind of snake-centaur, there wasn't any genitalia to give me any kind of idea about gender.

The worst part about the dreams was how it looked at me. Those blood-red eyes always burned into me, seeming to look directly into my soul, and its eyes told me that it liked whatever it saw in me.

I'D BEEN on self-proclaimed bed rest for four days when there was a knock on my bedroom door. I was so out of it, I almost didn't know where it was coming from. "Yeah," I said finally, figuring out the knocking wasn't just in my head.

Shelby walked in with a cup of tea from a nearby cafe. "Hi, Avery. I thought I'd drop by."

I'd been ignoring all my calls and texts, hoping the entire thing was a fever dream that was going to go away when I woke up.

"Your parents say you haven't been to your classes, how are you feeling?" The worry was painted all over her pretty face.

I shrugged, sitting up and trying to pat down my bedhead. She handed me the cup in her hand and I took it, grudgingly grateful for her kindness. "So, there's no chance that all of that was some long-winded bitchcraft dream?" I sipped at the tea, burning my tongue.

Shelby shook her head. "No, but it's not all bad. You make it sound like the end of the world. And it's not that, not for you." She took my hand and squeezed it, giving me the bright smile I loved so much. "Not for us."

I couldn't think of any way that I could maintain my relationship with her while I was effectively some demon's meatpuppet. "I just don't know how I feel about the idea of, you know, not being me."

It might have seemed like I was just giving in, but I just felt so foggy. I was unsure of so much, and a part of me felt like I was still in a dream. What was the point of fighting if it was all a dream? "The *Naga* doesn't take over the host, it *fuses* with the host, Avery. You *will* be you. You'll just have the power to do anything you want."

I shook my head, trying to organize my thoughts. I felt like she was still talking, and I was missing what she was saying. I tried to tune back in. "Babe, you can't turn your back on this. It's too big, it's too important."

I swallowed the tea in my mouth, burning my throat. "Not to me, it isn't. It's not my fucking demon god! You know I love you and I'll do almost anything for you, Shel, but taking a demon into my body just because you say it's an honor is kind of where I draw the line. It's *my* body, and I'd like to stay the only person in it." My anger was clearing the fog, but as soon as I felt it, I was already clouding over again. I tried to cling to the fleeting clarity.

"But Avery, how fucking cool is it that out of all of the seven billion people on the planet or whatever, you're the one that he *wants*." She looked like she was getting ready to start gushing over my 'honor' again.

I stopped her before she could. I might have been able to get her to tell me a detail or two about this demon-thing, but I wasn't sure I wanted her to. I'd already made my decision.

"Shelby, I can't do this right now. I don't feel well. I just...can you go? I want to finish this tea and get some sleep. I'm hoping to get back to classes tomorrow and forget about this whole mess."

Shelby looked at me, and for a second, I thought she was going to cry. She took a deep breath and blinked her shining eyes before leaning in and giving me a kiss on the forehead. "Okay, Avery. Call me later, okay?"

THE NEXT DAY, I got myself out of bed and dressed. I couldn't keep missing class, even if my head was so fogged up I could barely tie my shoelaces. I might even stop by the mall after work and find out what was going on there, whether I'd missed any shifts I'd been scheduled for, or if I even had a job anymore.

I checked my phone on my way down the stairs, saw an urgent text message from Shelby telling me to meet her at the mall. Part of me wondered if it was something about the snake-thing again, but even through the text on the screen I could feel something was off. There were no emojis, and I'd *never* gotten a message from her without at least one stupid yellow head in it.

I had to get to the mall.

I entered the Tavistock Galleria through the entrance closest to my store and rushed through the hallway to get inside. I ignored the greeting from my coworker as I made my way quickly through the store, dodging tables, displays, and customers, fighting against the cotton in my head with every step. I found myself at the door to the stock room, and I flung it open, racing inside.

She was panicking, all right. And for a good goddamned reason, too.

The thing from my dreams, the black snake-human *thing*, was more solid than I'd ever seen it, along with Shelby and a handful of employees from other stores. My first thought was what in the hell a cult meeting was doing happening at ten in the morning. It was a fleeting thought, though, as my eyes continued to scan the room. Next to Shelby lay what was left of Constance. It wasn't much, mostly a pile of gore and bones. It looked like her ribs had exploded outward, some of her viscera staining Shelby's clothes.

She stopped shouting when she saw me, and her eyes widened in shock and fear. The creature turned to face me the moment the door slammed shut. My breath caught in my throat and I was sure I was about to scream.

It wasn't exactly manly, I know, but what else are you going to do when there's a nine-foot monster directly in front of you? Try to fight it? I was willing myself not to piss my pants while trying to figure out how to get out of this mess without ending up like Constance.

At least Shelby was safe, since its attention was now fully on me. Now, I was born and raised in a city, so my survival instincts were not nearly up to par. My sarcasm, however, was usually right on the money, so when I opened my mouth and finally managed to choke out some words, I half-expected them to be my last.

"I thought you needed a host, tough guy."

Great, I was going to be remembered for *that* shitty one-liner?

Quicker than anything I could have stopped, the creature moved, sinking its fangs into my forearm. I'd tried to dodge out of the way, but it moved faster than my eyes could track. I had a feeling it had been aiming for my neck, so I'd at least done something right, even as pain seared through my forearm. My body felt weak. I felt the venom thickening my blood. My vision started to fade, and I hoped I would at least be unconscious for the worst of it. I looked to Shelby, still standing in the corner next to what was left of my manager, her face in her hands. I opened my mouth to tell her I was sorry I couldn't save her, but nothing came out.

And then the world faded away.

WE OPENED OUR EYES, and the first thing that registered was

the muted tones of the stock room. There was a dull, throbbing chant coursing through the room, urging us awake. What time was it? Part of us wondered if the mall was still open, or if the fusion had taken longer than anticipated. We took to the rest of our senses slowly, registering every part of our body as though it were the first time. Though, for one of us, it was the first time in centuries. We started with fingers, then toes, arms, legs, and finally, we put it all together, using muscles that were so familiar yet so alien to push into a sitting position.

The chanting stopped. We saw the mall-workers, our followers, all bowed before us. Except for the one, who still lay on the floor, nearly invisible to our changed eyesight as her body heat faded. She had spoken against our choice, had spoken against us, and had proven her disloyalty to the Nest. We looked at our body, clad in black clothing and ripped jeans; we touched the smooth flesh that masked the diamond-hard scales beneath the surface. We ran our tongue along the roof of our mouth, feeling the changes that had taken place there; the canines, now razor sharp, the venom sacs in the roof of our mouth, all hidden behind an attractive face and a smattering of rebellion. Our new visage was an illusion of teenage outrage that was sure to gain a following, if used correctly.

We got to our feet, walked through the silent, bowed forms, until we found the one we sought. Walking was a skill that the *Naga* was not used to, but the host carried him easily through the crowd until we found her.

"*Stand,*" we said to her, our two voices perfectly in synch. The woman did as she was told, hardly hesitating, though she reeked of fear. This was what she had wanted for us, after all.

The next time we spoke, the *Naga* held back, letting the host speak to his loved one unaided. "Hey, Shelby."

Tears streaked down her face as she held out her hand, unsure if she should touch us, or if it would anger us. The host was now fully in control of the limbs, reaching out for her to draw her close. "You were right, Shel," we said, pulling her into a tight embrace. "This is pretty fucking cool."

I SMELLED EVERY ONE

# I SMELLED EVERY ONE

By P. F. McGrail

MALLS HAVE EVERYTHING, DON'T THEY?

So why ever leave?

People toss out the phrase "homeless" with such cavalier disregard for what the term *actually* means.

I'm not homeless.

The mall is my home.

THE TAVISTOCK GALLERIA in West Mifflin, Pennsylvania has been my everything for nearly a decade.

My day begins before dawn. The JC Penny has just so many delicious little nooks and crannies that allow me to make a nest. Do you ever think about what's in the middle of those circular racks in the clothing section? It's a perfect place for me to hunker down all night on a bed of unsold women's pants. Mmmmmm.

Everything's put back in place before the first employees arrive, of course. Can't have anybody knowing about my nest, now can we?

I know what you're thinking. Wouldn't it raise suspicions if they found me wandering around before opening?

Not a chance. That stolen mall cop uniform has paid dividends many times over.

And Joe, the idiot night watchman, never suspected a thing. I would occasionally pretend to be a mannequin in the display case shadows, but his brain was dimmer than the after-hours lighting.

Maybe that's why he disappeared without a trace. I never did find out what happened to him.

And they never did replace that one. $913 a month was just too high a price for the Tavistock to monitor itself, it seems. What a sorry state.

I'm polite when the situation necessitates it, and send a 'good morning' wave to Urusla each day when she comes in to open.

You see, once a person *accepts* anything as a routine part of their life—be it a car, a rule, or a smiling man in a mall cop's uniform—they stop questioning *why* that thing is there in the first place.

That fact has sustained me for years.

Breakfast! There used to be an amaaaaaazing Cinnabon in the food court. Hell, there used to be a food court. Now there's just a creepy-ass carousel that children are rightly afraid to touch.

Forlorn, I'm stuck munching on cold cuts sandwiches, remembering the intoxicating aroma of cinnamon and warmth that would greet my day with all the sweet calmness of a warm blanket. For the record: fuck Amazon and your destructive, mall-crushing greed. Malls used to have everything, you see.

I could pass the days just getting lost in Tavistock. I'd browse the Dick's (Sporting Goods, you pervert), imagine that I had enough money to buy everything in Jimmy Jazz, and just stand outside the Bath & Body Works... *Smelling.*

There was nothing like the Victoria's Secret, though. I would come in and pretend to be looking for a gift that I could bestow upon my lovely "wife." Really, I was pre-shopping.

Sneaking into a lingerie shop after hours is *much* easier than you'd think, as long as you live in the mall. I was like a kid in a candy store. And to answer your question: yes.

I smelled every single item in the store.

You might be wearing one of my pre-sniffed garments right now!

I promise you that it passed the sniff test.

*Smelling.*

But I still have to toss things up every once in a while! That's where the holidays come in. I've pilfered a Santa uniform, a bunny outfit, several elf costumes, and a large dog-like getup that has no real explanation.

Again, I've become such a fixture that people just accept my presence. I can spend an entire day in the middle of the mall, greeting children and being photographed by their smiling parents! No one doubts the authenticity of a mall Santa!

Not even when I smell their kids' hair.

Now I know what you're wondering: could something as wonderful as the Tavistock mall *really* be in jeopardy?

I'm crying as I write this, because the answer is 'yes.' As the final doors close for the night, I prepare for bed knowing that I will soon *actually* be described as "homeless."

What a sorry state.

While I walk down the abandoned central walkway (avoiding the Hot Topic even at night, because those people freak me the fuck out), I head to the seldom-used utility closet for a midnight snack.

His glassy eyes take a moment to focus on me when I open the door. When semi-consciousness floats back into his brain, the young man is once again seized in terror.

Fortunately, he can hardly budge against his restraints. The boy's mutilated hands wouldn't do him any good, anyway, because his fingers were the first to go.

I pull out the carving knife, and slice a nice, thin layer of cold cuts from his belly.

Sure, I complain about my sandwiches. But when the meat is fresh, cold cuts really aren't that bad at all.

Oh, boy! It's a good thing that I knew how to slice out his tongue and sever his vocal cords, or he'd be making a racket! And you know what?

That tongue made a *good* fucking sandwich.

I pocket the cold cuts and the knife before closing the closet door on the convulsing boy. I do feel bad for him.

Because this is what happens when you're homeless.

THE DECISION IS FINAL, and it's nearly enough to shatter my heart:

The Tavistock Galleria is closing forever in June.

We all knew it was coming, really. But I didn't want to believe it. I couldn't.

Though keep in mind that it's *nearly* enough to shatter my heart.

But not quite sufficient.

See, malls have everything—don't they? So why *should* I ever leave?

I can't find a reason, either.

But what I *can* find is another mall!

So I'll be searching the country for the best possible fit. Nearly every major metropolitan area has one!

I will search until I find one with everything I need: a Cinnabon, a department store, hidden corners, lots of children. Hopefully not a Hot Topic, but beggars can't be choosy!

Smell you soon, folks.

# THE CAROUSEL OF TAVISTOCK

# THE CAROUSEL OF TAVISTOCK GALLERIA

By Candice Azalea Greene

A LONE WOMAN AND HER THREE-YEAR-OLD DAUGHTER CROSS the stained carpet outside my railing. The girl notices me and reaches out with one tiny hand. Eyes glued to the phone in her right hand, the woman senses the girl's desire to be put down and complies. She holds her daughter's hand to keep her from running away. Since the girl has short little legs, the two walk at a much slower pace. Her free hand stretches toward the fence encircling me.

I wink at her with a single light, she squeals with delight. A notification dings on the woman's phone. She releases her daughter's hand in order to reply, fingers flying over the touch screen. Expecting the girl to keep up, she continues walking. I play a few bars of "Kiss Me Again" to keep the girl's attention.

Making every effort to impress, I turn on the lights that currently work across the rounding board. Only ten light up. Back in my prime, every part of me worked as perfectly as the day it was manufactured. As long as I have joy and happiness from children to feed on, I can sustain my entire being and no need for a mechanic. Since Tavistock Galleria fell out of fashion, I haven't had the fuel to keep my gears turning.

I don't know what to do if this doesn't work.

Sunlight filters in through the grime-covered skylight above my rotund body. The windows haven't been cleaned in months due to budget cuts and lay offs. The light that filters through the muck is just enough to spark off my light bulbs. The merry tune of "Kiss Me Again" continues from where it left off, igniting a fire in the girl's eyes. She toddles over to a gap in the fence, reaching out for me with both hands the entire time. Just before her little hand closes on a drop rod, her mother swoops out of nowhere to snatch her up.

"Good thing, too. That rusty piece of junk is known to randomly turn on when least expected. It could've gone too fast and spit *la niña* out the other side." The mother eyes me warily before turning to the one janitor still employed at Tavistock: Anita, the tottering old biddy who has never cleaned the greasy fingerprints of dozens of kids from my poles or horses. She will hand scrub the blue porcelain fountain at the opposite end of the mall but can't be bothered to wipe down a few metal poles. That wetback needs someone to put her in her place.

Anita ushers the mother-daughter duo away. She glances back once and whispers something in Spanish, probably a prayer because she crosses herself afterwards. I want to scream in her face. I want to rage against her with human fists. I want... I want...

Bulbs wink out. The music doesn't fade; it halts all at once. Even the light from the skylight melts away. Drowsiness overcomes me. Who knows how long I'll sleep this time.

Will I ever wake, or is today the day I come to an end?

∼

"Giddy up!"

Darkness beckons, the seductive call almost too much to bear. It would be so much easier to give in, to become one with the nothingness.

"Giddy up, dammit!"

Sunlight filters onto the top of my metal-plated cap. It's warm, soothing—lulling me back into slumber.

"Worthless piece of shit."

Movement on the white stallion with the blue eyes. A shifting in weight as someone—a person!—slides down Monte Carlo's side. Sleep still threatens to overwhelm, but I have to fight back. I have to give this boy a ride.

It is a boy! He's not young, yet isn't quite an adult either. A teenager—still a child that I can glean energy from.

If I can just…yes! A single light bulb crackles to life, loud in the still air. The boy stops and looks up. "What the…"

Keep it up. Find the energy. My life depends on it.

A spark of hope is all I need.

I seize onto it before the boy can step off the platform. "Kiss Me Again" plays feebly. The boy grips a drop rod as he turns back to the stallion. Mustering the energy from somewhere deep inside, I move Monte an inch upwards. Heeding the call, the boy climbs back into the saddle.

His hope is my hope; his energy feeds me as the platform rotates a little: completing the circle. The burst of joy from his heart is enough to get me going. More lights flash on, although not as many as I would like. The music picks up speed, nearly getting up to its regular tempo. Monte moves up and down on his cranking rod, at first with a screech of metal parts that goes away as we continue to move.

The first ride any of us has had in weeks lasts less than five minutes. My platform holds fifty horses and fifty riders and consequently needs a lot of power to work properly. One boy on one lone stallion—no matter how prolific Monte Carlo once was—is not enough to keep me going. The boy's disappointment mirrors my own.

In the not too distant past, I was once the talk of the town. Parents would bring their children to the mall just to see me and wait in line for hours to take a ride on my mares and stallions. The original craftsmanship of the wood had been restored when I was built. My horses had been assembled from all corners of the country into one authentic piece dating back to the 1800s. I am the oldest carousel in the United States. Once I was the glory of Tavistock Galleria.

Now, I have become as derelict as the gated shops around me.

"That's it?" the boy complains. He slaps the side of Monte's head. A shudder runs through me. The boy jumps in his seat. But I have nothing left. What little energy I was able to glean from him was spent powering his short ride. I blink a light at him a few times to let him know I am still here. If he told his friends and brought them with him next time, I could go for longer. We could become friends.

"What a stupid piece of shit." The boy spurs Monte's sides. When nothing happens he slides to the platform and turns to leave.

As a last resort, the door to where my main bearing is housed swings open. Light sparks off the metal bars inside as I pour the last of my energy into the bare bulb that lights the tiny room.

**VCA Silver Lake Animal Hospital**
10726 19th Avenue S.E.
Everett, WA 98208

Dear Miriam,

Healthy pets make us happy, and we know they make you happy too! Our goal is to keep your pet in great health by providing scheduled wellness care on time.

Millie is due for:

Leptospirosis Vaccine 1/18/2019
Heartworm RX Refill 1/28/2019
Flea Prevention Refill 1/28/2019

We look forward to seeing you soon.

**VCAsilverlake.com**

© 2018 VCA Inc.

**CALL US TODAY FOR AN APPOINTMENT!**
**425-337-1500**

\*\*\*\*\*\*\*\*AUTO\*\*ALL FOR AADC 980
wk78 20181231-01 000159047-L5     305/3/
Miriam Brady
5128 137th St SE
Everett, WA 98208-9536

PRESORTED
FIRST-CLASS MAIL
U.S. POSTAGE
PAID
PET PORTALS

# Hi Millie,

## It's time for your Leptospirosis Vaccine

**Call us today!**

VCA CareClub.

"Huh?" the boy says rather intelligently and turns at the sound of the door creaking open. He looks over his shoulder then wanders inside me to have a look. The door shuts too fast this time to make much sound. My metal casing muffles the boy's cries. There is no one around to hear him anyway, not in a near-abandoned mall.

This type of energy isn't joy, it won't sustain me. Without joy and happiness, I slip back into sleep.

"It's been one week since the disappearance of Daniel Sanders. On July 26, Loralei Sanders dropped her son off at Tavistock Galleria for a few hours while she ran errands. How was she to know it would be the last time she would see her boy? Workers at the handful of remaining stores recall seeing Daniel wandering the aisles. He was like any other child in Tavistock—there only to look, not buy. The workers soon lost interest in Daniel. No one knows what happened to the sixteen-year-old. With its imminent demise looming on the horizon, Tavistock claims another victim. In November of 1987, Susanne Clomiskey was abducted from the galleria…"

The reporter's voice is cloying. Her sentiment may seem genuine but in person, I can tell you it is not. To her, this is work. A missing teenage boy is news, nothing more.

Being ripped from slumber by that voice has me out of sorts. I had been dreaming of a day long ago when Monte's white coat was brand new. It was his maiden voyage. His first rider was a seven-year-old boy with dusty brown hair and dark brown eyes. Oh, the joy horse and rider had felt that day in 1806.

Virgins bring the greatest joy. If I had ten virgins to ride me now, I would have enough energy to last me the rest of the year. There is something about a child's first carousel ride. The trepidation of being so high off the ground, the blaring, overly cheery music, the bright lights winking overhead. Then the jolt in the belly when the horse starts moving up and down as the platform rotates in a circle. While subsequent rides still hold some of the magic, they can never quite capture the ecstasy of the first.

I wonder, can Reporter Jillian smell the boy?

My stationary body must be in the background of the cameraman's shot. I can see the back of Reporter Jillian's blonde head. She missed a spot while curling her hair this morning. The long, main hallway of the mall is open. Those on the second level can watch the shoppers milling about on the ground. Skylights are evenly spaced down the length to let in the maximum amount of light. Strange smells wafting down the corridor could be coming from anywhere. A rat could have been stuck in a store and died from starvation. Anita could have mixed the wrong chemicals, sending mustard gas seeping through the still air.

No one has to know it isn't a rat's body decomposing behind a gate. Without children around to ogle my rusting poles and flaking horses, adults don't give a carousel a second glance.

"That's a wrap," the cameraman says and begins to dismantle his equipment.

"Good. Let's get out of here," Reporter Jillian replies. Her body twitches with the shudder she is repressing. "This place gives me the creeps." She glances around the upper level then the ground. Her gaze slides right over me. "I feel like someone's watching us."

"Kidnappings always give me the willies," the cameraman

agrees. "And this place isn't helping. Why don't they just tear it down and build another movie theater? God knows this city needs one. Cineplex is going to cave in during a movie one of these days."

Reporter Jillian laughs—genuine emotion this time—and says something I can't hear. They are moving away from me and sleep coaxes me once again. If only someone could do something about the smell.

INTERMITTENT FLASHES of real life dot my dreams of the past. Henrietta's rider clad in a Victorian high-collared dress of blue silks becomes the three-year-old girl Anita had whisked away before I could take her. A ten-year-old boy in a newsboy hat riding Don Juan and spurring his black coat becomes a small boy wearing cutoff jeans and a yellow-striped tank top standing outside the fence at Tavistock, face pressing through the bars like a squashed melon.

Sleep is fitful when the stench of rotting flesh permeates your insides. I wish I had arms to scoop Daniel up and toss him in Anita's trashcan to be taken out like the rest of the refuse. Reporter Jillian had been the only one to show up. Two weeks after Daniel disappeared, and the mall is as quiet as ever. I guess it's going to take something more scandalous to get the world to take notice of my dying home.

Waking becomes harder as the days pass. Sometimes I think I can hear children laughing and running about. If I manage to become coherent enough during these moments, the sounds fade and I realize it's all in my mind. Dying is rough. Without energy to sustain me, I am slowly losing my mind.

I don't want to die.

∼

Two towheaded brats follow behind a short, plump woman with matching hair. Their features are indistinguishable, except for a small brown birthmark on the chin of the child on the left. Her sister whacks her across the back when their mother isn't looking. Birthmark immediately begins screaming bloody murder. The mother absently tells them to stop.

"But, Mo-om! Sarah hit me!" Birthmark wails, fat tears cascading down her rapidly reddening cheeks.

"Did not!" Sarah counters. She stamps her feet as they walk, shouting out with each step. "Did not! Did not! Did not!"

"That is enough!" the mother shouts over them both. The two look mollified for the briefest of moments. Simultaneously, their mouths open to scream, but their mother stops them with an overdramatic gasp and loud clap of her hands. "Look! A carousel." She points at me.

No lights are on. Music doesn't play. I'm trying to look as inconspicuous as possible. I know what children such as these do when their parents aren't looking: they scrape the paint from my horses, kick divots in my platform, and write nasty words on my mirrors after fogging them over with their sticky, hot breath. Children such as these are parasites that need to be eradicated.

"It's broked," Sarah complains.

"Nonsense. It probably just needs quarters," the mother retorts. "Come on." The twin brats reluctantly follow her through the gap in the fence and up to my side. The mother makes a complete circle around me; the brats stay where they are, Sarah repeatedly kicking the edge of my platform with a dirty sneaker. "Huh. I don't see a place to put quarters in."

"That's because it's broked," Sarah mumbles.

"That's too bad," the mother says, truly sounding disappointed. A pang of something like regret passes through me. Even if I could work for her, she is too old to get any energy from. The brats might sustain me for a few hours at the most, but I don't want their kind on my horses, much less anywhere near me. If I could slap them away right now, I would.

The mother turns to the girls with a delighted expression on her face and claps her hands again. "Why don't you two stay here and play while I run into Penney's to pick up my pants? It's just down there." She points to the big white sign over the entrance to JC Penney several hundred feet away. "See?"

"This thing is dumb," Birthmark says. She is gripping a drop rod with sticky fingers, smearing it with filthy fingerprints.

"It's a carousel," the mother says as if that explains everything. "When I was your age, grandma would take me to the carousel in Central Park. I could play on the horses for hours, going round and round, until I made myself sick." The glimmer in the woman's eyes strikes a chord deep within me. Don Juan sits a little straighter on his pole, and I catch a fleeting image of a young girl who looks a lot like the brats sitting in his red saddle, laughing and screaming with the purely innocent joy only children can feel.

In response to the hope I feel from Juan, a light above his glorious black mane flickers to life for the briefest of moments. That's the only energy I can muster. But it's enough to catch the mother's attention. She waddles over to Juan's side, a meaty hand going to his flank and gently sliding over his body and up to his face. He nearly shivers with anticipation. He remembers her!

My horses come from around the country. Don Juan had been decommissioned from Central Park in New York City in the early 1990s, just a year after this woman had last ridden him. He had sat in storage for nearly a decade before someone found him. A master carpenter sanded him down and repainted his coat then sold him to the buyer who created me.

Tears leak from the woman's eyes as her hand rests on Juan's broad nose. If he were a real horse, he would butt her hand with his nose and demand a carrot. Perhaps this woman could be the next sacrifice.

"Fine," Sarah says, kicking Henrietta's pole and shattering the moment between her mother and Don Juan. The woman looks at her daughters and smiles.

"I used to ride this one in New York." She glances back at Juan. "I wonder how he got here."

"Just do your stupid shopping," Birthmark says and turns away. She walks amongst the horses, arms outstretched to run fingers over their sides as she goes. I hope she gets a sliver.

"I'll be back in just a few minutes," the mother promises. With one last glance at Juan, she turns and heads for the open maw of the store.

"How does this thing move?" Birthmark asks as she continues walking around the platform. She notices Henrietta's dappled coat and stops to trace the odd-shaped spots.

"Like I said," Sarah says in a smug voice, "it's broked. Why doesn't anyone ever listen to me? I obviously know the mostest."

"You don't know nothing. You're the dumbest," Birthmark

says with a smirk. She's not about to let her sister outdo her in the conceited department.

"You're dumb," Sarah retorts.

The intelligence of these six-year-olds is astounding.

"I'm telling Mom you said that," Birthmark whines.

I have never wished more for eyes to roll or hands to bitch slap than I do in this moment. Two children will make more of a headline than one alone. However, I don't want to put up with their mindless banter for nearly an entire week.

Allowing them to play on the platform and with the horses is excruciating. Even for six-year-olds, they are rough. Paint chips where they scratch at the horses with their feet when climbing into the saddles. Wood creaks under the weight of their hands pounding on the horses' heads and bodies. None of us is as young as we used to be. We have become even older without the joy of children to sustain us. If these girls aren't careful, they might break something beyond repair.

Once the hitting of each other's faces, and subsequent screaming, starts I have decided to do it. These are the first children that have been by in three weeks. Another store closed in those twenty-one days. If something isn't done soon, we will be left to starve.

The door to the gear housing slips open. At first, the girls don't notice. They are still too busy slapping each other. Sarah hits Birthmark so hard she goes flying and trips over an indentation in the platform, falling through the open door. The screaming immediately stops. Sarah takes a few steps toward the door and calls to her sister.

"You have to see this!" Birthmark shouts.

And with that, I have them. The door closes behind Sarah and just like before, they don't realize what has happened, until it's too late. The mother will never find out what became of her little girls.

THERE ONLY TWO times of year we can count on shoppers—during the months of October and December. Spirit uses the month before Halloween to set up costumes, decorations, face paints, and who knows what else in one of the empty stores. For the past five years, they have chosen to use one of the bigger stores on the second level. Rainbow used to be in that spot. That was one of my favorite stores because it sold women's *and* children's apparel. That's a magic combination. Being able to shop for both at the same time appealed to many women when the store was open. And that meant dozens of children passed on their way to the escalator. When that store finally shut their doors is when I began to feel the pull of oblivion.

Spirit has been open all of six days, and I have already collected four children: a twelve-year-old fiery redhead who hasn't stopped beating her fists against my insides, an eight-year-old autistic boy who likes to count my gears repeatedly, a five-year-old black girl who does nothing but cry for her daddy, and a two-year-old boy whose mother swears she only looked away for a second but was actually too busy swapping spit with a man old enough to be her father to notice her son wandering away. Surprisingly, no one has heard either the spitfire or the banshee yet. Neither of them will be able to keep it up much longer though.

The two-year-old was the first to die, the crying girl will be next because today is her fourth day without food or water. Although she's been crying nearly nonstop in those four days, tears no longer leak down her face. Even now, her whimpering is slowing. Soon she will join the two-year-old, the towheaded twins, Daniel Sanders, and a thirteen-year-old girl who surprised me by prying my door open before I was even aware of her existence.

She had tried to run when she saw the bodies of the others. By then, I was awake—mostly—and already had the door closing behind her. It was unfortunate her arm got caught in a gear. Really. Dying from shock is a horrible way to go.

Reporter Jillian has been by twice in those six days, and she has started to bring friends with her.

"This is Janet Ramos with Channel 11 News…"

"…Burt Kostas with Pittsburgh's Action News 4…"

"…Karla Walton with Fox 53…"

Jillian: "…where four children have gone missing from Tavistock Galleria in six days…"

Karla: "…Parents are keeping an extra close eye on the kids as they shop for Halloween costumes…"

Burt: "…The managers of Spirit have been interviewed by police. It wasn't until the store opened that kids started to go missing by the half dozen. Police are keeping tight-lipped about their ongoing investigation, but the managers of Spirit have been allowed to keep their store running…"

Janet: "…Sanders and the Thompson twins still remain missing. If anyone has any information on the disappearance of these seven kids, please call the number on your screen…"

Four reporters from four different news stations. It's a modest start, but I have twenty-five days until Halloween. Plenty of time to shock the rest of the world, as long as I can remain awake. Not only is the darkness' hold over me getting stronger, sleeping allows me to escape the crying, the screaming, and the death moans of those inside me.

∼

"Keep walking. Nothing to see here." The petite Mexican woman's grating accent pulls me from the clutches of nothingness. I think I had been dreaming of Henrietta's birth. There was a tree, a man, and an ax. Then the man was in a workshop carving a chunk of wood. Although I hadn't seen the finished product, somehow I felt it was attached to Henrietta.

"But I want to ride the pony!" a young voice retorts. I don't know where the speaker is. Even Anita's position is beyond me. Darkness still has me in its embrace. I can struggle, but we both know it's futile. I will be gone soon.

"You can't," Anita states unkindly. "It's broken. Out of order. *Lo siento*." She doesn't sound the least bit sorry to me.

I can hear the footsteps of many people on the carpet outside my fence. Only Anita and the child get close. When the smell of decay permeates a dying building patrons aren't too fond of spending much time inside. Management has blamed it on rats. The creatures have been infesting the closed stores for months now. They try to get rid of the bodies as soon as the rats die from ingesting poison, but the smell lingers. There was also the dozen or so leaks that sprung up with the last fall thunderstorm that rolled through town. Deodorizers and air fresheners can only do so much. If it wasn't for the business Spirit brought in and the police wanting to catch the perpetrator, the mall would have been shut down weeks ago.

"Life's not fair. Better get used to it now," Anita says. The child goes running back to their parent, somewhere amongst the shoppers moving to and from Spirit.

"I won't let you take anymore," Anita whispers as she steps close to my fence. She will not get any closer, I know that. If she did, I would take her too. Because of her, I haven't taken any children in days. Anita knows who the kidnapper is, but she's smart enough to keep her mouth shut and stay away from me. No one will believe her fanciful tale of an evil carousel that steals children; it's an absolutely absurd idea.

"You may look like a toy to everyone else, but I know what you are." She says something in Spanish and steps away from the fence. For days, she has been prowling around my perimeter instead of doing her work during business hours. Eventually, mall management will tire of her idleness and fire her. Eventually, the children will have no protector, and I will be able to take so many bodies they'll no longer be able to fit inside me.

Then the world will know.

Eventually.

~

WHISPERING voices wake me from my slumber. It usually takes loud noises or people talking for several minutes before I'll stir, but for some reason, tonight I wake fully and within seconds of the first voice.

"She's crazy, man. This is the dumbest idea ever," the second voice replies to something I didn't quite catch from the first speaker.

"If you don't believe it, then why don't you touch it?" the first voice says, full of derision.

Two teenage boys stand outside my fence. A third person

—I think it's a girl, but it's hard to tell—stands in the shadows under the overhang of the second floor. The first boy steps through the gap in the fence and stops next to my platform. He turns to the second boy. "See? Nothing to fear."

"Then you touch it, if you're so brave," the second boy says. His voice doesn't contain any of the taunting the first boy's had.

"Maybe I will," the first boy says. He glances at the girl and grins. If I could laugh, I would. Boys do the stupidest things to impress girls. That is one thing that hasn't changed through the centuries.

Let him come. Let all three come. I have room for them all in my little cubby. Maybe they'll even be kind enough to stack the other bodies to make space for more children. And best of all, Anita isn't here to stop them. She thought it was safe to go home for the night. After all, with the stores closed and the doors locked, who would want to enter a mall with nothing left to give?

The first boy takes a dramatic step onto my platform. When nothing happens he shoots the second boy a look and steps the rest of the way onto me. I don't react—no flashing lights and no cheery music for these three. One: I don't have the energy to muster up either of these things, and two: I don't need gimmicks to catch them when they're stupid enough to climb over me on their own.

Soundlessly, the door to the gear room cracks open. It's on the opposite side of where the first boy stands, but once he walks around, he'll find it. And once he doesn't return from that side, his friends will investigate.

"Oh, gross," the boy says when he reaches the other side and the smell hits him full force. "What died in there?" He steps toward the door, not a care in the world, and pushes it open. "Oh my god!"

"What?" the second boy calls, still on the outside of the fence. "What is it?"

"Ho-ley shit! You have got to see this. Meg, come here!" The girl starts at her position next to a column. She shakes her head, opens her mouth to speak, and closes it without saying a word. The first boy pokes his head out from behind the center housing and gestures for them to join him. "She was right! That crazy custodian was right! They're here. All of the missing children are here."

"What? Are you sure?" the second boy asks, taking an involuntary step through the fence, and that much closer to me.

"Dude! Some psycho's been stashing the kids' bodies inside the carousel. No wonder this place stinks to high heaven," the first boy says, a bit too enthusiastically. Why are teenage boys especially fascinated with dead bodies?

"We should call the police," Meg says from her spot by the column. She's the only one who hasn't moved this entire time, except to wrap her body more tightly around the plaster.

"Not before we check it out," the first boy shouts back. "You coming, Dex?" The second boy turns from Meg's direction and nods at the first boy. "Sweet! What about you, Meg?" The frightened girl shakes her head and slips further behind the column so only her head and fingertips show. "Fine! Be a chicken. Hopefully the sicko behind this isn't out there in the shadows waiting for us to turn our backs so he can take you too. Who knows what he'd do to a pretty thing like you." Meg squeaks and quickly looks all around her.

"Not cool, Blaize. Can't you see she's scared enough as it is?" Dex scolds. Blaize doesn't look abashed; I don't think he knows how. Dex shakes his head and turns toward Meg. "Come on. Don't listen to him. The guy could still be here, but if you're with us, he can't hurt you. I won't let him."

"Ooohh," Blaize coos. "Dex finally grows a set. Think Meg will like you now, hotshot?" Dex shows no indication that he has heard Blaize. Instead, he walks away from me. Meg meets him halfway. He takes her hand and leads her back. I can hear him calling Blaize a dick under his breath. Meg only nods. She has his hand in a death grip. Too bad they won't make it out of here alive. It looks like Meg really could fall for the boy willing to go up against an unknown assailant. Soon they will realize just who the assailant is. They won't be able to do anything about it by then.

The pair steps onto my platform at the same time. Dex pulls Meg behind him and escorts her between the horses until they are standing next to Blaize. Meg throws her other hand over her nose and gags.

"That's the most horrible thing I've ever smelled," she complains. She draws the collar of her star-spangled black shirt over her nose and holds it there with her free hand. "Let's do this and get out of here. This place gives me the creeps."

"Check this out," Blaize grins and leads them into the cramped room. Meg keeps half of her body in the doorway so I can't close the door yet. She chokes back a scream and steps closer to Dex. He wraps an arm around her shoulders and pulls her even closer. If I attempt to close the door now, I might knock her enough that it will close—if I can get a good amount of force. On the other hand, she might get caught and the boys will easily be able to pry the door open and escape.

I'll wait then.

"Don't touch them!" Dex shouts, and everyone jumps.

Blaize swivels toward the couple, his flashlight shining directly into Dex's face. "What the hell, man? Are you trying to give me a heart attack?"

"You can't touch the bodies. The police will look for fingerprints. What do you think they'll do when they discover yours? You're in their system. They'll have no problem matching them," Dex explains.

"So?"

"Dude! They'll think you're the killer!"

"You really are dumb," Meg says, shaking her head. Her eyes flit to the door. If Dex weren't holding onto her, she would probably split. I have to get the door closed, before the boys make the same decision.

Blaize snorts and turns back to the bodies. "I knew that. Anybody have a pair of gloves?"

"Why do you want to touch them?" Meg asks, her voice full of contempt. "They're dead!"

"I know. Isn't it cool?" Blaize grins at the body closest to him. I think it's the black girl what wouldn't stop crying.

"They were once real live human beings. Human *children*." Meg is quickly losing interest in the situation. I need to do something to get her far enough inside that I can close the door.

Summoning as much strength as I can, I pour it into the lights, the music, and the platform. Three lights switch on. They're faint, but in the darkness of the mall, it's like lights over a football stadium. "Kiss Me Again" echoes in the stillness for a few seconds. The horses move forward an inch then stop. Everything shuts off again, the music dying as it spreads through the empty mall. But it was enough. Meg had jumped into Dex's arms, and he instinctively pulled her back and into the room.

I shut the door, sealing the teens to their fate. It's a good thing the mall is currently closed because three teenagers screaming at the tops of their lungs would definitely be heard by patrons. By morning, they'll have worn themselves out. Their vocal chords will have been exhausted, and then in four or so days, they will join the rest of the children in eternal slumber.

"With the body count now over ten children, citizens of West Mifflin ask when it will end. City and state police are doing all they can to catch the Tavistock Kidnapper, but is it enough? Some are asking for help from the federal government. Only time will tell if their cries will be heard."

It isn't Reporter Jillian's voice that wakes me—or any of the other Pennsylvania reporters. Someone new has come to town. Dredging the last remnants of sleep from consciousness, I open myself to my surroundings. All of the previous news reporters are here. I can see them standing yards apart from each other as they talk to cameras. The woman whose voice woke me looks more official than the others. Local reporters lack the panache of the better-known reporters. She's from one of the stations that broadcast nationwide. I recognize her voice now; I have seen her on the TVs that used to be placed around my perimeter for parents.

Finally, I am getting the recognition I deserve. Finally, the people of West Mifflin will see me; they will see me and fear me. They will flock to the mall in droves to see the carousel kidnapper. Perhaps they will change the first letter to make it into one of the catchy titles humans adore so much: The Karousel Kidnapper. I like it. People from around the world will know what I did. Visitors will frequent the mall, the shops will re-open, and life will resume its merriment. My horses and I will flourish. We will give millions of children joy and happiness, and in return, they will share theirs with us.

After all, giving joy and happiness to children is my only mission in life, my only reason for being.

A PUNGENT AROMA rouses me from deep sleep. There was a man dressed like the American Indians I've seen on TV movies. He was standing next to a burnt pile of wood—Monte's once white face blackened and cracked—screaming at me in his native tongue. I don't know why, but I felt like it was a warning. The black-haired man was trying to tell me something, but the acrid smell woke me before I could figure out what it was.

Words in a different language fill the hollow space of the mall. The reverence…the cadence… Although I don't understand this language anymore than the Indian's, I know the speaker. I come fully awake as I realize what Anita is doing. Piles of firewood lay under every third horse. The mall custodian walks along the platform dousing the stacks in gasoline, and leaving trails leading from one pile to the next. The words she speaks are a prayer.

Curse the god she prays to, and curse this infernal woman! Without hands or a body to move, there is nothing I can do to stop her from burning me alive.

"Are you awake?" Anita calls to me. "Can you see what I'm doing?" A shudder runs along the platform, vibrating the mounds of wood. It isn't enough to shake them free. "Good. You will no longer be able to hurt anyone. Your days of death and evil are over. Do you hear me, *carrusel*? You are finished." My platform bucks in response, throwing the *puta* off balance for a few seconds. She grunts when gasoline sloshes onto her shirtfront. "You can't get rid of me that easy. I know you're dying. You don't have the energy to stop me." She falls silent as she continues her work.

Standing several feet from the edge of the platform, Anita removes a small box of matches from the breast pocket on her striped work shirt. Even when she's not working, the blasted woman wears the same shirt—the shirt she would wear over the uniform the mall had given her, and wouldn't take off no matter how many times they demanded it. Why this of all things irks me beyond reasoning, I can't say.

This can't be the last thing I see—the demon woman ending me before I've truly begun my work. The worldwide coverage had just started. With only one person here to witness my downfall, the world will never know it was I who kidnapped West Mifflin's children. I—not a man—but me: a carousel, an inanimate object. I would've blown the minds of conspiracy theorists and ghost hunters around the globe.

"Freeze!" a sudden voice commands. A man dressed all in black, including helmet and goggles over his eyes, steps out from behind the very same column where Meg had cowered all those days ago. Long, black guns peer out from behind every column in both directions, going back into the darkness until I can't make them out anymore. "Identify yourself."

Anita freezes with the match poised over the striker on the side of the matchbox. She glances at the man, squinting to see him in the dark night. "Who are you? What's going on?"

"Pennsylvania State Police. You are under arrest for breaking and entering, vandalism, and arson. Identify yourself," the man commands again. He doesn't advance on Anita, none of the police officers do. I guess the idea of going up in flames doesn't appeal to them either.

"Anita Lopez. I work for Tavistock Galleria. Well, I did, up until a week ago." She points at me with her thumb and forefinger, the match still held between them. "This thing is the culprit you want. It has been stealing the children. They're inside the compartment in the middle. Open the door. You'll see I'm telling the truth."

The man perks up at the mention of the missing children. His shoulders hunch as he takes aim at Anita with his rifle.

"No, no," Anita yells, "I didn't do anything wrong." She points at me again. "That thing did it. Check inside. I promise you'll find the children."

"Ms. Lopez, I need to you step away from the carousel, drop the matches, and slowly turn and lie face down on the floor. We'll take you down to the station and get his whole thing figured out." The man spoke slowly, enunciating his words with care.

Ha! He thinks she's the crazed killer of Tavistock. The look on her face is worth twenty children. I flash the ten working lights, momentarily blinding the men in their night-vision goggles. Shouts ripple to either end of the mall. The man who had been talking to Anita snatches off his goggles. He blinks rapidly, trying to clear his sight.

"Oh, no you don't," Anita growls and brings the match to the box again. She flicks it across the striker, an orange flame immediately igniting. I blast music; Anita flinches but doesn't stop.

Panic from fifty horses explodes within me. Some of them are over 200 years old. The trees they had been carved from probably no longer exist. Progress bulldozed over them decades ago. They are relics, from a forgotten age where joy and happiness could be found by riding in a circle on a stationary horse.

Screams of pain erupt as the fire burns its way across my platform. A gunshot—or is it a part of me exploding—echoes through the mall. Although once lustrous with paint and lacquer, the wood has slowly been rotting since Tavistock started dying. The horses burn easily. Their charred remains fall to the platform where large holes open.

"What the hell is that?" one of the men shouts from behind a column. They stagger around, guns knocking against their hips, as if in a drunken stupor.

Even police officers aren't immune to death cries. It isn't just the pain from the horses. Hundreds of children have sat on my steeds. The joy that has sustained us all throughout the centuries is astronomical in numbers. What little joy that remains inside them, burns hotter than their own pain. Their cries of anguish as jubilation turns to torment are more than I can bear.

The fire's part of me now. I can manipulate it with what little energy remains. Anita got gasoline on her shirt. She will burn as well as any of us. I shoot a string of flames toward where she had last been standing, but she isn't there. She's lying on the ground as commanded. When the flames fall on her there are no screams of agony. A bullet-shaped crater sits in the middle of her chest, bright red blood trickling down her sepia skin.

"Look at the carousel!" a man shouts. All eyes turn to me. In my rage, my door popped open. Through the flickering wall of flames, fifteen bodies of children ranging in age from two to sixteen can be seen lying haphazardly within my depths.

"Jesus," the first man—the man who must have shot Anita

because he's the only one still holding his weapon—whispers. "They've been here the entire time. She stored their bodies inside the carousel and blamed the smell on the rats."

As the men gather closer, they stare at the fresh body burning on the floor. "Why do you think she did it? Was she mad at the mall for shutting down and wanted revenge?" one of them asks.

The first man shakes his head. His rifle finally lowers. He holds it to his hip, as do all of the men. "I interviewed her myself. Back when the first boy disappeared. I had forgotten about that until she said her name. She seemed perfectly normal, never even made it onto the list of suspects. We only interviewed her because it was procedure to talk to all mall staff."

As one, the men turn their attention back to me. The children are burning now. Their death cries happened long ago. Only my horses can be heard, their keening fading as their lives extinguish.

"My God," the first man says. "The bodies were inside the carousel this entire time."

Darkness, my old friend, is that you? I can feel your tendrils snaking into my consciousness.

Light from the fire is nearly gone. I can no longer hear the crackle of burning wood or the voices of the SWAT team. Only emptiness remains—a vast expanse of nothing.

Black nothing.

Nothing binds me to my horses anymore. Are they too lost within the ocean of oblivion? With only eternity ahead of me, perhaps I'll be able to find them and reunite the carousel.

If I strain hard enough, I think I can hear Monte Carlo calling for me.

Somewhere, far away in the void, my horses wait for me.

# DESTINATION

DESTINATION

By Ashlyn Walker

I WOKE UP HERE THREE DAYS AGO, BUT IF IT HADN'T BEEN FOR the sun shining through the broken windows overhead, I would have lost track of time by now. I have no clue how I got here. I have no clue how to leave. If I'm being honest, I don't even know for sure if I woke up, because when I realized where I was, it was as if I gathered my bearings while I was already standing; like the fade-in to a movie or something.

I was strangely unafraid, like I had a purpose here that I couldn't quite grasp. It was more like a video game than a movie, I realized, but my objective was muddled and shrouded in a fog. I felt a disconnect from the me I had a vague memory of, and a stronger connection to a stranger buzzing in my mind. I didn't have the mental power to truly question what was happening, what had happened already, I was wholly focused on this feeling. I had a strange, or maybe not so strange at all, feeling that I needed to do something here. Like there's a puzzle to solve, a mystery to unlock. There certainly was a mystery.

And where is here?

Well, I quickly gathered after walking around for the first hour or so that I was in an abandoned mall. Long abandoned, judging by the ivy that snuck in at the doorways that I somehow could not pass through. The floors were dirty. Shelves that still lined the walls in some of the stores held random knick-knacks left behind, obscured by an inch of dust. Some of the stores were blocked by gates that I could only look through, while others were differing degrees of accessible depending on how ajar the old, rusty gates were. Still others were completely open, gaping mouths as entrances, not at all inviting as they would have been in the mall's heyday. Some of the store names were still legible, but most of the neon had been smashed by vandals and no memory of former occupants remained.

I explored the whole mall on the first day, and have done so several more times since, but that first day is when I found the map. It had what I assumed to be the name of the mall at the top: "Tavistock Galleria." Other than that, the map was basically unreadable, covered in grime and worn down. The name meant nothing to me, and I wasn't even sure if I was in the same state I had been before waking up here. I concluded I must still be in America, at least, but not knowing my exact whereabouts was unsettling.

I didn't mind most of the mall, though the overall atmosphere was anything but positive. But when I discovered an old and very faded carousel, the paint on the animals chipping off in strange patterns, I felt such a disturbance that I fled from that area of the mall altogether. My preferred place that I found to rest and wait, to think, was what must have at some point been a fountain; a wishing fountain, I'd hoped. I pictured the fountain full and active, copper shimmering at the bottom of a pulsing pool. I enjoyed imagining that area had life, but the fountain wasn't my favorite part about this quiet place. When I laid on my back inside of the fountain, I got to look up at the large colorful stars that hung overhead. I concluded that these were the least affected by the mall's closure and abandonment and I felt safe beneath them.

It occurred later to me that this may have been a risk on my part. I wasn't sure about their integrity as they hung from the ceiling, but I had no fear that one may fall on me. Looking at them brought me great joy, and I found myself spending most of my time here, on my back, imagining I heard the fountain running, pretending the stars were twinkling. The sun was beginning to set now, as I lay here, and I grew sad as I realized that this meant no more light to view the stars, as it had been for the first two nights.

I didn't feel tired, and I hadn't felt hungry. This should have been more upsetting to me, as these were natural functions that I was always used to experiencing, but I explained it away as a side affect of shock and confusion. I refused to acknowledge that those emotions were also absent. My thoughts began to wander, and it occurred to me to think: *Am I still a human being?*

I held my hands in front of my face and considered them for a long time. I saw them; five fingers on each hand, pale peachy skin...the same as they had always been. But somehow, they were alien to me. I touched my fingertips together first, and then my palms. I felt myself, but the sensation was almost as if I had learned what feeling my skin had felt like, not like I was feeling them now. Though this revelation was immediately unsettling, my mind quickly moved on and I dropped my hands to my sides once again.

Was this self-preservation?

Before I could answer my own question, a loud sound, compared to the all-consuming quiet, filled the space around me and rang in my ears for several seconds. It was a heavy metal door, I realized, and it echoed through the silent mall. Now I had movement in my limbs, a real purpose. Now I could feel my heart pumping, a sensation I hadn't realized was absent until this moment. I was supposed to figure out where that sound had come from and who, or what, had made it.

I boosted myself up off my back, ready for action, but I hadn't had the chance to move from where I stood when I saw it. A figure stood across the way, perhaps 100 feet from me, completely still. It was silhouetted by the fading light from the evening sun. I didn't have the chance to be frightened. I knew that I needed to approach, needed to investigate, and my feet were moving before I directed them to do so.

The figure began moving away.

"Hey!" I shouted. "Come here. Let me talk to you. Who are you?" My feet weren't listening, but my voice was. Curiosity beat out fear by far, and I didn't care if this thing was a threat. It was human, or humanoid at least, and I sensed that if it came down to a fight, I could take it.

To my relief, amazement, and then, horror, the figure spoke. At least, I think it did. They did... *Something* did. The sound came from where the figure stood, but there were way too many voices for the one body. They spoke, all layered on top of one another, "You will know. Tonight. You will discover. Are you ready, Benjamin?"

The shock of hearing my name was drowned by my immediate sureness of my answer, "Yes." I said, confidently. I continued moving backward, the figure mimicking my movement back out the door from which *they* entered. I chased after them, but when I got to the door I was greeted by a heavy chain and padlock barring my way to the thing that had spoken.

Lights suddenly filled the space around me, and noise. It was the mall, but different. So different. It was alive. The fountain behind me bubbled to life, the stars above shone more brightly than they had. Groups of people that hadn't been there moments before laughed, grumbled, talked to one another and walked along either side of me. They walked in and out of stores, all open, full of commodities and in perfect condition. The floor was polished and shining like new. The sudden light and noise was so overwhelming, but once I had regained my bearings, I looked closer at the faces in the moving, pulsing crowd.

Was this real?

I watched them, but they did not watch me; did not acknowledge my presence as they went about their business. And then I realized: They were not walking along either side of me, they were walking *through* me. I attempted contact.

"Hey, can you...can you see me?" I began shouting it at everybody who came near, but nobody acknowledged me. Nobody could see me until one voice, that was actually several voices, filled my ears.

"Do you understand?" The voice asked.

I could not see the source of the voice anymore, and I grew increasingly frustrated. "No, I...what is this?" I felt a thought beginning to tickle at the back of my mind, raising my hairs on end, but it never had the chance to grow.

"Move." The voice said, and I obeyed without a thought.

I joined the flow of the crowd that moved around me,

through me. I didn't know where I was going, but I knew not to go into any of the stores. That's not where I was needed. I needed to move forward. After 15 minutes of walking with the crowd, back and forth, retracing steps and traveling in circles occasionally, I looked up and realized where my intuition had brought me: right in front of the carousel I had avoided when the mall was in its decrepit state.

There was nobody riding it, yet it turned; the animals now shiny, rising and falling to the rhythm of the cheerful song that played far too loudly. I wanted to get away. The ride was no less unsettling in this light. My feet, though, remained planted and after a few minutes of staring, the voices returned just behind my back.

"Watch," they said, "Just watch. Don't look away. Watch."

"Okay," I wanted to say, "Okay I get it."

The voices continued to insist that I watch carefully, but I couldn't move my mouth, couldn't move my body. All I *could* do was watch. And, so, I did. And there they were.

Small bodies phased into my view as the carousel turned, rising and falling, rising and falling. There were children who hadn't been there a moment ago. "What is this?" I wanted to say. I wanted to say it, but I still had no power to control my body.

"You see them." The voices said. "You are ready. Now, close your eyes."

I tried to obey. I tried to say that I couldn't move, I couldn't close my eyes, I couldn't speak. The children, I realized, were no ordinary children. I already knew that, but what I witnessed next was garish and explained my hesitance to be anywhere near that damned carousel. They seemed to change before my eyes. Their clothes were rags. Their skin was a different array of colors: green, blue, pale ivory white and ebony black. They were in different states of decay, I realized, and I felt like I may be sick, but I still could not tear my eyes away or close them. And then they looked at me, my heart racing, attempting to break through my ribs and get away. They looked at me with empty sockets where eyes should be. They pulled me in, and everything went black.

I was at a gas station. It was late afternoon. The sun was golden outside of the windows. I was here because...because I was visiting my ill mother and she wanted candy. She was suffering from dementia, had had a stroke last month and was trying so hard to get it together. I was in a state that I wasn't familiar with. Where was I? School had just gotten out. I had taken a cab to get here, they were waiting outside. No...I hadn't made it to the gas station. I was going to the gas station, but when I tried to picture the inside, I couldn't. I tried to picture myself handing the candy to my mother... which candy had I bought? I hadn't had the chance to buy anything because...there was screaming. So much screaming and screeching and the smell of alcohol. I remember my cab driver hiccupped when I got into his cab. The smell of alcohol...had I not noticed? The school bus was going along on the opposite side of the street, the cabbie was driving too quickly.

"Hey...hey buddy, would you slow—"

And that's when it happened. That's when the screaming started. That's when I knew I had made a horrible choice, he had made a horrible choice. We were going into the other lane. We were in the other lane. We were on a bridge. We weren't on a bridge anymore, we were in water. There were five children, they were almost home. They were almost home but they didn't make it.

They all died. I died.

When I opened my eyes again, eyes I hadn't remembered closing, the carousel that had just been in front of me wasn't there anymore. It was a space, empty and discolored where a carousel had been a long time ago. It was empty, save for five children, each one sopping wet. A tall man, a protector, the bus driver, stood next to them with his head down in… shame? And there were hundreds and hundreds of people gathered around us, watching…waiting.

They knew what was going to happen now, they knew what I was about to find out. They all seemed expectant and I realized the truth, then. This was the domain of the dead. How many abandoned malls, airports, office buildings…how many decrepit, forgotten buildings house forgotten souls? It was being fed to me like a thumb drive plugged into my skull.

I knew everything, I knew how each one of these hundreds of people around me had died. I knew the story of this place, how it had fallen to a shamble. I knew the life that once filled this place, and the death it itself had experienced. Sadness consumed me knowing all of these things I hadn't known or didn't want to know. It only made sense that this is where we would gather…places like this. I fell to my knees, trying to understand, trying to figure out if this is really how the story ends.

The hand on my shoulder, the owner of all of the voices, spoke. And when he spoke, I could taste the alcohol in his breath.

"Now you understand." It said. And anger bubbled up in my stomach and filled my chest with a heat that I could not sustain. It was the cab driver.

"You Killed them!" I shouted as I turned and swung with all of my strength, my voice working sufficiently now, but I fell to the ground in a great heap instead of connecting with…the man?

"All in a day's work." The voice said, almost cheerfully, then chuckled. He had moved back several hundred feet in a second's time, bowing, "Welcome to your final resting place, Benjamin."

# THE END OF TAVISTOCK

# THE END OF TAVISTOCK

By Elizabeth Davis

My morning routine of watering and whispering to my upside-down tomato plants was interrupted by a knock on my door. Looking through the peep-hole, I was quite confused. The other person was a perfectly put-together business woman with a sensible dark blue dress. Her blonde hair pulled into a tight bun, and she was giving my door a suspicious look. She didn't look dead. Not that ghosts always looked dead, but she lacked that wispiness that marked even the most alive looking ghost.

I opened my door, nervous with this change of routine. Her frown deepened as her blue eyes looked me up and down.

"Are you Dr. Ashes?" Disbelief dripped from her voice.

"Yes. Not many people call me that. You can just call me-"

"Dr. Ashes is fine. We need to talk inside - privately." Her tone let me know that she wasn't going to brook any argument. Deciding I wasn't going to fight this until I figured out what was happening, I let her in.

"Sorry. I don't get many visitors," I apologized as I cleared cactuses and books off a chair. "Do you want something to drink?"

She gave my apartment an appraising look, and chose to stand, despite her high heels. "I would prefer to get down to business right away."

I bottled up a sigh and listened.

"The head of the Medium Volunteer Association referred me to you. I need someone to help clean a commercial property of… *ghosts*."

She said the last word with so much distaste, I wondered briefly if 'ghosts' was her secret code word for incompetent baristas who put milk in soy lattes.

"We can't even conduct environmental testing until it stops being haunted. The new batch of inspectors are coming tomorrow."

"That doesn't sound like one of our normal cases. Most of our cases involve helping out people who are too poor or too dead to afford the normal rates."

"I found the regularly available mediums insufficient to the task. I explained my situation to the head of the association and after a significant donation, they agreed."

I thought of the robed figure, worrying over the demolition of rows of abandoned apartments, trying to find new homes for the spirits that gathered there, along with the annual ceremony to soothe the ghosts at Arlington. Of course they took the offer.

"Here are the details of the property." She handed me a manila envelope. "I need this matter handled with the greatest discretion. It would harm our reputation if this embarrassing incident were to come to light. Especially to potential buyers."

"I'll try to get this soon. It may be a little tricky with work."

"You aren't working today. I need this matter dealt with as soon as possible, understand?"

I had plans, though. These consisted of a dinner of listening to W complain about American Chinese food, and then settling down for a double feature of Jackie Chan films at a small local theater. And for the record, I personally like American Chinese food because it's well, food, but I *love* Jackie Chan movies. Therefore, I was tempted just to tell her to go and get chased off a cliff by a herd of bison. But...

How Blowing Her Off Could Go Wrong:

1. The Head of Mediums Volunteer Association will get annoyed at me and he is not subtle.
2. This could cause Jess to get involved because she has no sense of boundaries, and that possibly could end up with parts of Washington D.C. being set on fire.
3. Okay, I'm going to be honest, she hasn't set anything on fire recently, and has never (to my knowledge anyway) actually committed any arson in Washington D.C. I reckon she's had to be more subtle under Lady Leon's watchful eyes. But the Head of the Medium Volunteer's Association wasn't known for her subtly.
4. Except for that one incident with the flying guillotine blades.
5. And that other one with the defenestration.
6. Okay, so this could still end up with the shit hitting the fan. And if it hit the fan bad enough, the news could reach my grandparents all the way back in the Hopi Nation. And they would call me, and if they

found out it all happened because I shirked my duty-
7. Yes, because the only reason you shouldn't be a terrible person is because your grandparents will scold you. Seriously?
8. This is hardly someone in dire need. They just can't sell some property because of a few ghosts who are probably just peacefully haunting the mall.
9. You still have your duty to those in the mall—they may need your help.
10. And what if there is something more there than just a few ghosts, and that's why those other mediums passed it up?
11. What's the worst that could happen anyway?
12. Missing out on my evening plans.
13. Getting soaked in pea soup.
14. Getting seriously hurt
15. Which could result in the embarrassment of having to call Miss Morgan to regrow my arm again and interrupt whatever she's doing today.
16. Even worse having to wake up in the hospital and call her because I hate hospitals.
17. If it's really that dangerous, better me than anybody else, right?
18. Sigh.

"I reckon I can fit it in tonight."

"Excellent. I expect that you will live up to your reputation. Just one question."

"Yes?" My hope that she would be leaving soon were dashed.

"Why do you choose to live in a building that's so hard to

get to?" Annoyance tinged with genuine curiosity broke through her strictly business tone.

"You could've just called," I replied, trying to throw in that angry bite that Jess used to end conversations.

"This meeting was too sensitive to allow for anyone to overhear," she told me in a tone that let me know she thought she was talking to an idiot. Clearly, I had failed. "It doesn't change the fact that I had to come here before the sun rose but after midnight because the moon was waning—that's what the instructions said. What sort of apartment building is this?"

"Well, it's actually a hotel that burned down a few years ago."

She stared at me for several seconds, not sure whether or not I was being serious.

"How does that relate to apartment buildings that have existential problems?"

"It's still the hotel. That's why it looks so fancy."

"So, they rebuilt the hotel, and?"

"This is the ghost of the hotel that used to be here." Her eyes went wide, and she began glancing around nervously. "You see, everything has a soul. Items that have strong emotions and memories tied to them, such as happiness and sadness develop an even stronger soul. That soul may be able to continue after the destruction of the physical being. That's why the Titanic keeps sailing although all of her passengers decided to move on. Or you can still find a certain tea house during cherry blossom season that burned down during the great fire of Kyoto…"

She gave me the "I'm fed up your American Indian Hippie Bullshit" look - as my last boyfriend put it.

"Maybe you should think about spending more time around the living."

"Hey! I spend time with the living almost every day!" She ignored my protestations as she left my apartment, pushing her way past the puritan Abigail, still playing on her Gameboy. Which earned her a glare from Abigail's hominid canine guardian, who had been Abigail's pet dog in life. As the elevator doors closed on my unasked for new client, I reminded myself that I wasn't doing the job for her.

AFTER HOURS ON THE ROAD, I was in a pretty foul mood. Once I'd found out that the mall was in Pennsylvania, the only way I could arrive in time was to call in a favor from a work associate. I wondered what the hell my reputation was that the woman thought I could just teleport down here.

I parked my borrowed flaming motorcycle in front of the mall's main entrance. Of course, the place had been closed for months, so the building was surrounded by a chain link fence that had been unenthusiastically assembled and was only tall enough to keep out very small children; unless those children were sort of determined, then they could get in too without much effort.

Preparing for the worst, I climbed over the gate and unlocked the front door. Before I even stepped onto the dusty tile, the ghosts swarmed; clinging to me with frantic desperation. Their fear of being caught in the mall leaked into me, along with the usual baggage. Maybe there were plans to demolish the mall—many ghosts find the destruction of their home to be traumatic, stemming from the fear of sudden dissolution to the other side or transformation into something worse. If I could help them, then something good would come from all of this.

Setting to work, I wrangled my power that was roiling with all of the sustained attention. Blowing across the top of my flute, I started a tune I had first heard my uncle play for us in the kiva and later for the tourists that came to the Moenkopi Inn. I sent it searching for any souls that were hiding, too scared to come out, hoping that the feeling of comfort would go to them.

Walking through the dusty mall, playing my flute while looking at the abandoned shopfronts—some of them still filled with signs and mannequins. As afternoon light filtered down through the skylight, it was actually relaxing. Until I heard someone yell "Who's there?"

As I turned the corner, I looked down at a circle of black robed figures around an empty fountain. Oh great, other people. It's always awkward to run into living people while I was working.

"I'm sorry. I didn't mean to bother you. I'm just here to collect some ghosts. Ignore me."

The leader, which I guessed from the golden pentagram symbol on his black robe, stepped forward. "You have seen too much, shaman, medicine man, witch, whatever your call yourself!"

"Don't call me a witch!" I snapped, taking the bait without thinking.

"Jesus Christ!" someone shrieked behind him.

"Mercedes, we are supposed to avoid such language-" he scolded as he whirled around and stopped.

"The fountain is spewing blood!" shrieked another.

It was true. Instead of water, blood splashed out, filling the stagnant air with a coppery smell. The robed figures huddled together, muttering about "Did we mess up the ritual?" and "Does this count as a sign of pleasure or displeasure from Baphomet?"

"Um, that was my fault," I said. "That happens when I lose my temper. Sorry. It should go away after a few minutes. Never had an issue with lasting stains."

The robed figures watched me with wide eyes as I got closer, none of them moving to stop me from analyzing their summoning circle.

"You mentioned Baphomet. You were trying to summon him or one of his underlings?"

"Yes—I learned the ritual from a vision I earned from diving deep into the tome of-"

I was too impatient to hear about whatever moth eaten counterfeit grimoire he had managed to get his hands on. "You should've done more research. Your Latin is just word gibberish, and I don't think you got any of the Enochian symbols right. You are just blindly fishing right now. If you caught anything at all it was purely accidental."

I looked deep into the chalk circle around the fountain, past the linoleum floor to the other side. I could see their energy as bright lines, thrown into the darkness of the far-off oceans beyond. The bright lines twisting away, leading back to somewhere on the surface. I crouched and pressed my hand into the center, letting myself travel down the path, connecting with other bright lines and found something climbing up them, consuming them, growing strong. A spirit came with the smell of popcorn, and greasy food, the sound of people talking, the sound of a cash register, of Muzak over a scratchy speaker, the unmistakable 'clank' of a Zippo lighter. . .

"Yep, you didn't get Baphomet. That's not his resonance at

all. He's all brimstone and hellfire usually. You might have gotten a minor underling with that spell. Which would still be unlikely, but it's been intercepted. It seems to be drawn to something inside the mall."

"It must be that damned Baal cult in the Radio Shack or maybe that coven from Hot Topic, or even the Dagonites in the food court..." the leader muttered to himself.

"Just how many cults are there in this mall?"

"This mall was built on powerful ground. Thus, many of us were called and we fight for mystic control of this space while it's still open to us. But it's to be sold soon. Probably demolished. So, we all have to make our final moves."

"What do you mean called?"

"We all have had dreams of this mall—of something great in this rotting shell that needs to be unleashed! We all dreamed of these halls, this fountain, the carousel, every crook and corner, every inch called to us! Isn't that why you're here?"

I looked down below me and wondered how long it had been sitting here, feasting on stolen worship. It was so close to surfacing, to taking back its old shell. "As I said, I'm just here for the ghosts..." The ghosts thrummed closer to me, their fear causing a noticeable drop in temperature. Whatever this thing was, it had the ghosts really spooked.

At that point, all the pieces clicked together.

"Oh horseshit!" I shouted as I dragged my boots across the chalk circle, breaking the connection between the cult and the giant soul beneath us. "Baalities in the Radio Shack, a Coven in the Hot Topic, and Dagonities in the food court—how many other cults are there in this mall?"

"Um, um, I think it's just those." He muttered, looking away from me.

"The blood is flowing in the fountain again," one of the other robed figures commented with resigned horror.

I turned to the ghosts around me. "All of you go and bring them back here. Please." I sent them flying on the words of "Don't Break My Stride." Hey, just because my grandmother had taught me using our traditional songs doesn't mean I always had to be traditional.

The cult shrunk back as the ghosts materialized, flying away on my power. Soon, screams echoed through the mall and I was satisfied with watching more of those bright strands snap away, even as the floor shook under me—that soul had been close to pulling itself in to the material plane, but for now it was still safely on the other side.

Within a few minutes, we were joined by a group of cultists in red robes, a group wearing fish masks, and the Coven, dressed in normal clothes. All of them were pulling in breath, giving nervous glances to the ghosts that had returned to hover behind me.

"Who brought a fishing pole?" one of the Baalites teased between huffs.

"At least they have a spark of originality," one of the Coven retorted.

"Well, if it's get cold, at least we can burn you witches."

"Excuse us for not falling prey to stupid clichés that were out of date before your grandfather's balls dropped."

"Robes are a classic."

"It's a rip-off of our look!" The Baphometites jumped in.

"At least we put in effort," the Dagonites said with a hurt tone.

I cleared my throat, trying to get their attention.

One of the Coven's members pointed their finger at me.

"You. . .you're the one who scared us half to death with your," she paused for breath, "Halloween store knockoffs."

"Hey! Just because Jones had a," I rummaged through my mind for the impulses of memory from my contact with the ghosts, "suffered a rather dramatic and improbable accident on the escalator doesn't mean you should say mean things about the way he looks."

Jones held up his head and shook it in the pantomime of a mournful nod.

"Neither did Heather ask for that stalker to stab her in the neck, nor anyone for the school bus crash. You know this mall has a surprisingly large number of ghosts for only being open for a few decades."

"Can you we skip all the creepy ghost stuff, and just find out why you brought us all here?" One of the fish-masked people asked with a muffled voice.

"Oh, yeah. So, you all need to stop having your rituals. At least in here." The crowd scowled. Both at me and each other. "I know you think this is all very powerful ground, but it's not. You've all been misled by the soul of the Tavistock Galleria."

There was a moment of stunned silence before "What the fuck?" was shouted at me by all the cults.

"It's not uncommon. Especially when a building has been left to decay before properly dying. It's just trying to bring itself back to full life. Reinvigorating its body. The problem is, that doesn't work. Given that most buildings doing this are usually, well, think of it as suffering from dementia. When it doesn't work, they tend react out of anger and confusion. Best case scenario is that it turns its anger on anyone that comes inside but it's still bound to its husk. Worst case scenario, we end up with a rambling mass of wood and stone that's a menace to everyone in the state of Pennsylvania."

I was greeted by an incredulous silence. One of the Baalities started to say something, before being elbowed by one of the Baphometites who pointed at the ghosts behind me. I sighed, remembering Miss Morgan's advice: "It doesn't matter if you're right, all that matters that the boyos behind you are bigger than the boyos in front of you." I felt the Tavistock Galleria's soul stir under me, and I looked down, to see one bright strand still reaching down to the broken pentagram.

"Is there anybody else left in this mall?" I snapped at the crowd.

They took a step back and exchanged nervous looks. Finally, one of the Coven spoke up. "Crazy Dave might be up on the roof again."

"Who in the hell is Crazy Dave?" The leader of the Baalities asked.

"He thought the mall was going to be the site of the Second Coming. He was up there at least once week, praying for hours. I took him a sandwich occasionally and talked for a bit. I think he's just lonely." The Coven member explained with a shrug.

There was a crash through the skylight further down the hallway, as a headless body splatted on the ground.

"Was that Crazy Dave?" I asked.

The coven member shook her head solemnly. "Oh yeah. Even without his head you can tell. He's always wearing that "I shot JFK T-shirt."

As the last of his life leaked away, the mall surged under our feet and pushed through to manifest. The building shuddered and shook around us, as the spirit took control over what remained of its body.

"Run!" I yelled.

That shook the cults out of their shock and into a stampede. They nearly made it to the exit, before the shopfronts slammed down in front of them.

The Tavistock Galleria roared: a high-pitched whine combined with the worst of Black Friday crowds. As the cults stumbled back, mannequins broke out of the shopfronts, the shattering glass crunching under stiffly lurching feet. The fountain darted away from us on a wave of plastic tile and wood; space folded, and it was replaced with the carousel- a carousel made of decayed and skeletal animals, their garish paint flaking off as they stalked from their wooden poles.

"So, this is the worst-case scenario?" The black robed leader panted.

"No, just medium. It's not yet mobile, it hasn't brought any other scavengers here to join the brawl, and there are no bloodthirsty Santas."

"That normally happens?"

"Psychic residue from all the screaming kids in Santa's lap."

"... Never mind."

I looked at the army of mannequins and decayed animals as the floor shifted beneath me. I felt the ghosts huddle along with the cults, both scared of being trapped forever in the mall's wrath. However, I could probably still escape. The cults —well I can't say that they were innocents. But the ghosts. . .to spend a near-eternity trapped in here, the mall harvesting them for energy until it finally broke down or was set on fire by a lightning strike. Even more so since Crazy Dave joined his ranks, his disappointment and confusion as he huddled with them, wondering where heaven's glory was. There were no angels or second coming here, only betrayal. A normal person may be able to walk away, but a person like me, they would always find me. Especially in my dreams.

This had gone beyond just a simple exorcism. If I had been smart, I would've walked in here better armed than just a flute and few knives. If I was even smarter, I would've brought one of my friends along with me.

But since I hadn't, I was going to have to take a page out of Miss Morgan's book and form a battle plan with ludicrous odds of succeeding. Miss Morgan, by the way, is an expert in surviving really bad situations, especially ones brought on by making unwise decisions, and her book is a great way to pass a rainy day, even if the closest she has to a book is scrawlings on bar napkins.

"It's probably best if you stay back," I told the group, trying to project as much confidence as I could. They gave me the look reserved for crazy people, and probably backed away due to the army coming at us rather than anything I'd said. Well, no time to worry about my poor social skills.

"If you don't come back," said the leader of the Baphomet cult, "We'll send the Dagonites after you."

"The hell you will!" Cried several of the Dagonites.

I squared my shoulders and rushed at one of the mannequins. It stumbled, off balance which made it easy to knock over. It might have been animated by the will of a malevolent mall, and it was certainly frightening as it shambled around mindlessly, but it was still just flimsy plastic. Kneeling over it, I pulled off the arms and legs with mumbled "sorry, sorry, sorry," as it flailed at me the whole time.

I lifted the mannequin's torso from the ground as its limbs crawled away. Holding the torso out in front of me as the army turned its attention on me and just me, I sprinted for the carousel. As planned, I was able to use the torso to deflect the claws of a decayed tiger before dodging an eye-gouging beak from an ostrich. The good news was that the mannequins were too slow to keep up, as I continued to move toward the carousel.

As the wooden animals continued to attack me, maiming the already mangled mannequin shield, I reflected that this was easier than expected. This was certainly no run in the caverns around the mesas I had grown up on, slipping on rocks and coughing on dust as I avoided skin walkers, witch's servants, and monsters spawned from Trinity. If nothing else, at least the decayed linoleum floor was still smooth and stable.

Within arm's reach of the carousel's controls, I threw the mannequin's torso at a horse rearing to rain its hooves down on me. In the brief reprieve, I hammered on the go button, feeling the controls hum and spark as the carousel started up. I jumped on and grabbed onto an empty pole before it fully took off.

This is what I know:

1. The mall had pulled the fountain closer into itself while it was awakening. Therefore, it was probably a weak spot, perhaps even the heart of the Tavistock Galleria.
2. It replaced the fountain with a carousel.
3. Therefore, there must be a connection between the carousel and the fountain, even a weak one, thanks to the rules of sympathetic magic.
4. Which means that I should be able to use that relationship to navigate through the body of the soul and find where the Tavistock Galleria had hidden the fountain inside itself.

As I held onto the pole, I could see the mall change around me. I saw the mall as it was when it was young, thrumming with life, people rushing from store to store while fake snowflakes forever fell from the ceiling. I saw a girl and boy laughing in the food court, the same girl stabbed and dying on the floor upstairs. Children in the arcade, shrieking with delight at a new score. Two girls, dancing in prom dresses around the carousel, as two become one

You know, the normal stuff you find in a mall.

Worried about being lost in the mall's memories, I crooned one of those sad country songs about looking for love in all the wrong places and won't it take to where I need to be? Slowly, it listened to my request, and I could feel my power surge, wanting to burn out of control and swallow this whole mall. I kept a tight grip, only letting it help sway the soul against itself.

I saw the mall in its wane, the stores boarded up, or being picked over by thrifty scavengers. Mall walkers circling around the fountain. A man chased by mannequins and two girls pursued by a giant cat. I felt the mall's sadness clutch at me, trying to lure me off the carousel into the emptiness around, as the last shop closed up and the entrances were locked.

Time and space further collapsed, and I was flung off the carousel, crashing into one of the walls of the fountain. Brushing dust off my shirt and massaging a jammed shoulder, I looked up at the fountain. It had grown bigger than the last time I'd seen it, stretching all the way to the sky light, multiple basins and pillars, all ready to catch flying water. But the water came low and intermediate, with not enough force needed for great leaps or gracefully falling down, instead just dripping on the cracked blue tile, leaving dark stains behind as the liquid slowly drained.

A wail blew out of the empty jets as the building shifted and groaned. The spirit knew that it wasn't well known enough, a place for work or shopping but mostly just passing through. It hadn't been allowed to stand out from the other malls, and nobody had invested enough in it for it to haunt after it's body was demolished. The Tavistock Galleria was dying, and it was scared.

I pulled myself up into the basin, boots splashing in the dirty water. My arms circled the main pillar, and I rested my cheek against the blue tile. It quivered below me, the water pulse erratic. It knew it was weak here, that it could not fight back without inviting its own destruction.

I've never had to sing a mall to its death before, and neither had my grandmother or my teachers at Miskatonic U. So, I didn't have a song prepared. Malls weren't a big part of my childhood; the few memories I had were of my mother tightly clutching my hand, so much that it hurt, me not complaining as I watched the dead creep closer and closer to me. Still, there was something I could use. A perpetual jingle played outside a Chuck E Cheese, the same jingle I hummed on the way back home. The Christmas songs played on repeat from October to New Year's. The Top 40 easy listening hits that were popular back then. I sang all of that as it came to mind, slow and soft.

For once, I didn't feel my power lap against me, trying to splash over my walls. Instead it tentatively reached out, as the mall grew quieter around me. I could feel the fountain shrink as the mall unfolded, space reasserting itself back to its previously known dimensions with a slow exhale through the jets.

As the cracking and creaking of space unbending ended

around me, the gurgling inside the pipes died away and the exhale ended. The tile grew cold against my cheek, and I let my words die away. The Tavistock Galleria had gone to wherever malls go after their death. Hopefully, it's a place with lots of customers.

"What are you doing?"

I looked up to see the cults standing on the cusp of fountain, with the discarded husks of mannequins and decayed wooden animals around them.

"Just helping the mall die." I responded as I pushed myself back up.

"So, we've been talking, and we think that we should just go ahead and head out. Leave you to do. . .whatever you're doing."

"Good idea, I agreed, "The mall—"

The walls shrieked around us as the skylight cracked and splintered. Without the spirit, age and neglect was catching up with the building. This time they didn't need me to tell them to run. We pounded across rotting floorboards, avoiding chucks of falling masonry as the building shuddered. We pushed through the rusted doors, too stiff for my key to work, having to rely on sheer numbers to break the unmoving hinges. As we stumbled over each other, I stopping to pull up a few faltering stragglers before the building gave its final shudder.

The good news was the motorcycle appeared on top of the rubble, as the building continued to cave in. My client was going to be furious, probably. But:

1. She had to give her donation before she even talked to me.
2. She had been rude.

3. She had only asked me to deal with their ghost problem, nothing else.
4. They were going to have to demolish the mall anyway, so I saved them time.
5. And if I hurried, I could still make it back in time for Jackie Chan.

The cult members stood around eyeing each other nervously, and none of them seemed interested in talking to me at all, and this suited me just fine. I rolled the flaming bike to level ground and checked to make sure I had enough gas to get home. Which was good because I had no clue what was fuel for this bike. I waved goodbye to the ghosts. Some were leaving to find out what was next after so many years being hidden from the light, while others linked hands to go and search the world for their next home.

PUBLISHER'S NOTE

Please remember to
**honestly rate the book** on Amazon or Goodreads!

It's the best way to support the authors and help new readers discover their work.

READ MORE HORROR

Read more horror from
Haunted House Publishing
and download a **FREE BOOK!**

TobiasWade.Com

Made in the USA
San Bernardino, CA
04 January 2019